D1524504

Adonis & Venus

A D.C. Love Story

By: TyLeese Javeh

Text **Treasured** to **22828**

To subscribe to our Mailing

List.

Interested in becoming a part of the Treasured Publications family?

Submit manuscripts to

Info@Treasuredpub.com

Ty Leese Javeh

Published by Treasured Publications

http://www.treasuredpub.com/

All Rights Reserved

All rights reserved. No part of this book may be reproduced, stored in or introduced into a retrieval system, or transmitted, in any form, or by any means (electronic, mechanical, photocopying, recording, or otherwise), without prior written consent from both the author and publisher except brief quotes used in reviews. The scanning, uploading, and distribution of this book via the internet or any other means without permission is illegal and punishable by law.

Acknowledgments

I thank God for all my blessings. My publisher Treasure of Treasured publications for believing in me. I would like to thank Royalty Publishing House for giving me this opportunity. Of course my wonderful support team my sister's Samantha, Sabrina, Ladonna Turner, and my daughter Tilysha. My pen sisters Ms. T. Nicole, Reign, Authoress Nicole Dior for allowing me to bother you daily with ideas or read this I stayed in you guys in box and emails. We pulled each other through the tough times and I thank you for being there and for encouraging and believing that I could do this. Ashley, Kevin, Andrea, and Keisha thanks for the many times I called, sent a text, or in box interrupting you at work with my thoughts and ideas for this book. A special Thanks to Jonathan Harris, without your advice, words of encouragements and pushing me out of the corner, I wouldn't have taking the initiative to take the time to better my craft. You didn't have to take time out for me but you did I appreciate you so much. To all the Authors in the Royal family thanks for the support and for all the readers thank you for getting to know me and supporting me as a new author.

A note from the Author

I didn't believe that I can write this kind of book, it was the one genre that I stayed away from. I wasn't confident in myself and I second guessed myself a lot. But I had a lot of people in my corner to encourage me and I appreciate them so much. No one had to take time to listen to me but all of them did. It's because of the many people that believed I could do this when I didn't that made this book possible. Thanks

Contact Ty Leese Javeh:

Facebook: tyleesejaveh

Twittter: tyleesejaveh

Instagram: tyleesejaveh

Wwwtyleesejaveh.webs.com

Synopsis

When Lavelle and Adonis's father walked out of their lives, Lavelle turned to the streets to help support his family. Proving that he is loyal and trustworthy, Lavelle quickly takes a seat next to the well-known king of the streets Frank Lewis as his right hand man.

Adonis has always looked up to Lavelle not only is he his older brother, but he's the only father figure he's had in his life. He taught Adonis everything he knows about life, the streets, and being a man. For Adonis, life was pretty easy but when he falls for a beautiful girl name Venus, he finds out how hard life can be.

Falling in love with Adonis was the best thing that happened to Venus. Growing up with an addict for a mother, she had to fend for herself and her siblings. Anything they needed she had to take care of until she met Adonis who provides for her and her siblings. As she grows into a woman, Venus wants more for herself. Struggling to build a career she finds that life in the DMV isn't all peaches and cream, neither is love.

As what seems to be a war on the streets is starting, Adonis finds it difficult to run his team, find out who is behind the war, and support Venus in her journey to build her career, which causes her to make a tough decision about their relationship. Adonis does all that he can to put the pieces of his relationship back together but is it too late?

With Trying to find out who's gunning for them, a growing romance between friends, a new love interest for Venus, and an unwanted relationship, Adonis must get his head in the game and his mind right before he loses everything.

Dedicated in loving memory of my mother Hattie Mary Hailey My cousin André Orlando Harrington Jr. My uncle Vernon Tyrell Cooper

To everyone in the world who lost a love one, they may be gone but the memory of them will never be forgotten.

Prologue

I got my gun, put it in my waist, and headed to the front of the condemned building. I walked in. Anfernee, one of the workers, was tied to a chair, blindfolded and gagged. I walked over to him and spoke to the nigga that was standing guard.

"So this lil' nigga was the one who set all that shit up?" I asked as I snatched the blindfold off. The nigga I was talking to nodded his head yes. I looked at Anfernee, who was sitting in the chair trembling with tears in his eyes.

"You stealing money from us, nigga?" I asked as I towered over him, ready to do some more damage to his already busted up face. He didn't respond. I started raining blows on him. I had to take it a little easy. I knew his lil' bitch ass wasn't working alone; he didn't have the heart to be the mastermind behind this shit. I hit him a few more times, then I needed him to talk.

"Anfernee, Anfernee, Anfernee, you really wanna give your life up for a nigga that wouldn't do the same for you? That nigga out here looking out for his fuckin' self. You were just a pawn in his game. You might as well make this easy on yourself; who the fuck are you working for?" I asked elevating my voice to put fear in the nigga's heart. He jumped so hard that he almost fell out of the chair. He was breathing rapidly like he was about to cry, trembling and sweating and shit. I pulled out a knife and pressed it under his eye. His breathing became labored as he let out a muffled yell. I removed the gag from his mouth.

"Scream all you want; no one can hear you in here. Now, this is the last time that I'm gonna ask you." I pressed the knife deeper into the skin under his eye. "Who the fuck is you working for?"

His wide eyes darted around the room as if he was begging for somebody to help him. I exhaled a frustrated breath. The look I was giving him must have alerted him to the fact that I was about to cut his eye out because he started to talk. His faint voice started cracking as he whispered the name. I didn't hear him, so I leaned closer and told him to repeat himself. His voice was slightly above a whisper as he called out.

POW! POW! POW!

Words can't a few explain the feeling I got while lying on the cold ground, bleeding profusely and choking on my own blood, knowing that I was about to die. I took quick shallow breaths, trying to get some air. I couldn't believe that after everything I had done for this nigga, he was the one to take my life. I chuckled at the thought as pain struck deep in my chest like a bolt of lightning. I started breathing more rapidly, trying to get through the burning sensation from the three gunshot wounds in my chest that were sending chills through my body. I started coughing and the taste of blood filled my mouth. I spit a big glob of blood on the floor, then laid my head back down. A lone tear rolled down the side of my cheek as I started to lose consciousness again. Every time that happened, I would think that was the end for me. I wasn't ready to leave my family, but death was coming, it was inevitable. I'd lived a hell of a life on the streets of Washington D.C. I'd done a lot of things that I knew could come back on me, but I never saw this shit coming.

"Out of all people, I can't believe it was you," I mumbled. "After all I did for you." I took another quick breath. "Karma will come for you too, trust me." I breathed.

I was pouring sweat as heat filled my body like an erupting volcano, and thoughts of my life flashed before my eyes. I had to drop out of school to help my family. We were struggling and as a man, I couldn't sit back and watch the people I love go without. I started selling drugs to support my family, but the money I was making only helped a little. The niggas on the streets took me as a joke 'cause I was a young nigga tryna make a come up. I felt like I had to prove myself, so I started grinding hard day and night. It didn't take me long to learn all I needed to know in this game and make a name for myself. I started making a killing; that's when niggas started to take notice of me. I was the muthafuckin' man and wasn't shit them niggas could do about it. I felt a lump of blood rising in my throat. I tried coughing it up but it wouldn't move. I knew the end was near. My heartbeat slowed down as my breathing became faint.

"Please forgive me." I whispered. My life flashed before my eyes one last time as I drifted out of consciousness.

A year earlier

Venus

Looking at the time on the clock that read 5:23 PM had my blood boiling. No matter how many times we'd had this conversation, it seemed as if it didn't mean shit to him. After calling his phone for the fifth time and not receiving an answer, I went from angry to worried. I got up and walked into our kitchen. As I walked around the kitchen sliding my hands across the marble countertops, I looked at the travertine floor and the stainless steel appliances. None of this shit meant shit to me anymore. My eyes darted around the kitchen and I noticed the meal that I so eloquently cooked, sealed in containers and placed on the stove for him, and I thought about everything I did to please this man. Frustrated, I grabbed two glasses and a bottle of Moët out of the under-counter built-in wine refrigerator. I headed to the living room to join Kay Kay, my best friend of 15 years. I gave her a glass as she looked at the time on her cell phone and rolled her eyes.

"See, this the bullshit I be talking about; he knew how important this meeting was to you," Kay Kay furiously spoke as she crossed her left leg over her right and started bouncing it angrily.

She was pissed the fuck off and I didn't blame her. Adonis was supposed to be home an hour ago to take over caring for our six-year-old daughter Harmony. I was late for a meeting with a clothing manufacturing company that was interested in creating the prototypes for the line of clothing that Kay Kay and I designed. This company was not only offering to make the prototypes, but they were giving us full use of their factory and employees for any future manufacturing needs. Being a fashion designer had been a dream of mine since I was a young girl, and Adonis knew how hard I'd worked for an opportunity like this. Kay Kay let out a loud sigh, then shifted in the dark charcoal recliner as I filled her glass up.

"This is so fuckin' ridiculous. You bend over backward to make sure he has everything he needs and wants, and you ask this selfish ass nigga for one favor and he can't even show up on time. But as soon as he wanna get his dick wet, yo ass gonna be right there spread eagle and waiting," she continued rolling, her neck and eyes.

"Kay Kay look, I'm as pissed off as you, but maybe something important came up." I shrugged my shoulders, hoping she would drop the subject but knowing her like I did, I knew that she wouldn't. Kay Kay was my best friend to the end, but she had no filter and sometimes her mouth was reckless. She said what the fuck she wanted, when she wanted, how she wanted, and didn't give a fuck who didn't like it.

"What the hell is more important than you and your needs?" she asked. She uncrossed her legs and scooted to the edge of the chair. She folded her hands in her lap and gave me a look that said *bitch please explain.*

"Kaylee, his lifestyle is unpredictable; anything can happen, you know that," I said with irritation in my tone. She was starting to piss me off even more. It was bad enough that my feelings were hurt, but her talking shit was like adding insult to injury and I was about a few seconds away from getting up and slapping the shit out of her. The fact that he wasn't there had me more worried than angry, and I had too much fucked up shit running around in my mind as it was. I didn't need her running her damn mouth.

"Girl, you sound like a fuckin' fool; ain't shit come up. Speak the truth. Ever since you had Harmony, yo ass been put on the back burner. He don't give a fuck about what you want, and this shit right here proves me right."

I was not in the mood to keep listening to her go on and on about my man, even though she was right. The frustrations in my relationship already had me questioning his love, and her little rant was adding to that. What she didn't understand was Adonis had been the one to have my back since the first day we met seven years ago.

* * * * * *

I was 15 and the oldest of three kids. My mother was a drug addict and would use all her welfare money and sell her food stamps to support her habit, leaving me and my little sister and brother with little-to-no food in the house. Whenever my siblings got hungry, they would get the saddest look on their faces that would break my heart. To make sure that I never saw those looks again, I would steal food to feed them. It didn't stop there. I started stealing any and everything else they needed. I was in the store on the corner of Nannie Helen Burroughs stealing enough food to last for a couple of days. Usually, I'd be in and out so quick that Mr. Li wouldn't even notice me, but that day was different. Mr. Li was slicker than me. I didn't notice him watching my every move until he yoked me up by my arm, making me drop my tote bag and spilling all of its contents on the floor. I started screaming for him to let me go. That's when Adonis came in.

"What's going on, Mr. Li?" he asked. He gave me the once over, then smiled.

"This girl steal from me." Mr. Li said in his heavy Chinese accent. I gave Adonis my best pleading look. Mr. Li

was trying to call the police and I was using my eyes to beg Adonis to help me.

"Hold up, Mr. Li; don't call the cops," he told him. He had one hand on Mr. Li's shoulder and the other on my arm. Mr. Li's eyes were darting back and forth between me and Adonis, as if he was tryna figure out what to do.

"Ok Adonis, for you.," he agreed, putting the phone down. He let me go and I tried to run my ass out of the store, but Adonis grabbed me up in his arms, lifting me off the ground.

"Wait shawty, come here." he chuckled, placing me down in front of the counter. "Why you stealing?" he asked.

"None of your damn business." I snapped as I snatched away from his grip.

"Look, I'm tryna help yo ass, the least you can do is calm the fuck down." He raised his voice and gave me the same rude attitude that I was giving him.

He told Mr. Li that he would pay for the items that I was stealing as well as anything else that I wanted. He gave me a jovial look, then told me to go get whatever else I needed. Even though I was skeptical about his intentions, I scurried around the store picking up the other items that I needed. I wanted to hurry and get as much as possible before he changed his mind. After paying for the groceries and passing me the bag, I made a mad dash out of the front door. I didn't realize that he was chasing me until I felt his strong grip snatching me from behind.

"Stop fuckin' touching me!" I shouted.

"Damn ma, calm yo ass down. What the fuck is yo problem?"

"Like I told you, none of your damn business." I sneered as I adjusted the heavy ass bag in my hand.

"Look, I'm tryna help yo lil' ass, chill the fuck out!" he shouted, then offered me a ride home.

"I don't know you. I'm not getting in your car." I replied.

"Girl, I just saved yo ass from going to jail. Get in the car," he demanded as he took the bag out of my hands. I slid in the passenger side of his black Ford Explorer. The leather was so hot from sitting in the sun that I felt the heat on my ass through my shorts. I tried to play it off, but my ass felt like it was on fire. Adonis put my bag in the back seat, then came to close my door.

"I'm not fucking you," I told him. He started laughing hard as shit. I, on the other hand, didn't see anything funny. I knew how these niggas were. They wanted to do shit for you to guarantee them some pussy, but I wasn't the one. Adonis stopped laughing, leaned over me, and the scent of his cologne engulfed me; it was intoxicating, I took a deep breath trying to inhale the scent as he looked me dead in the eyes like he was seeing right through me.

"I can get pussy anytime, from any girl; ain't nobody tryna fuck you. I just want to help you," he stated in a low, sexy voice. He put the seatbelt in the latch, then asked my name.

"Venus, but my friends call me Vee." I answered.

"So what do I call you?" he asked.

"Venus." I said with a turned-up lip and wrinkled nose. He giggled as he introduced himself, and that was when I noticed how extremely good looking he was. His skin was smooth and dark, like a Hershey's Special Dark candy bar. His jet black hair was low cut and shaped up to perfection, with more waves than an ocean. His matching jet-black, thick eyebrows made his deep-set, chestnut eyes sexy as hell, and his teeth were as white and bright as freshly fallen snow. To say he was fine as fuck was an understatement. I flashed him a beauty pageant contestant smile as he extended his hand for a shake. I took his hand, then told him that it was nice to meet him. He closed the door, went around the other side, and opened the door. I noticed him looking me up and down and licking his bottom lip as he slid in the driver's side of the truck. I blushed, then *chuckled a little. I adjusted the seatbelt to make myself comfortable as I called out my address to him like he was a taxi driver. When we arrived at my house, he gave me some money along with his phone number and told me that he didn't want me stealing, and that if I need something to call him. From that day on, Adonis took care of me. I never needed or wanted for anything, until now.*

* * * * * * *

"Kay Kay, please let's just drop this okay? I just wanna try to relax," I pleaded. I took off the jacket to my Armani light gray, skinny-leg pantsuit and laid it across the back of the sofa. I then kicked off my royal blue Manolo pumps and sat with one knee bent under me as I poured myself another glass of Moët.

"Ok Venus, I'll drop it. Besides, that nigga ain't gonna stop our muthafuckin' dream from coming true any fuckin' way," she replied, lifting her glass in the air and nodding her head before taking a huge gulp like she was taking a shot of Tequila.

"Damn bitch, this ain't no Patrón," I chuckled. She giggled a little, then gulped the rest of her glass down.

A few hours and another half of bottle of Moët later, Kay Kay was tipsy and ready to go home. I was a little more that tipsy; my ass was drunk. Staggering, I walked her to the door and gave her a hug goodbye. I locked the door, turned on the alarm, then carefully picked up Harmony, who was sleeping on the red nailhead chaise lounge that sat near the full length arched window, and carried her to her room. Making sure not to wake her, I changed her into her Disney princess nightgown and put her in her bed, then headed to my room to take a quick shower.

I watched as the clock changed to 10:34 pm and a worried feeling shot through my body. It wasn't like Adonis to go all day without calling me, or to not return any of my calls. I picked up my cell to check for any missed calls or texts, but there weren't any. I tried to call him again, but still no answer. I sat back on my customized, marquee panel, king-sized bed and turned on the TV, trying to get rid of the million and one thoughts that were now invading my mind. I started searching news channels to see if there are any breaking news stories, but there weren't. I then started calling hospitals and police stations to see if maybe he was injured or locked up, but he wasn't locked up or in any hospitals.

"This is driving me fucking crazy," I thought as flipped through the channels looking for something to watch. I needed something to rid me of the worried feelings that had my stomach in knots. I laid my head back on the headboard and started watching a movie on Lifetime. I was determined to stay awake until he got home because if he wasn't somewhere hurt, then there was no excuse as to why I hadn't heard from his ass yet, and that meant Kay Kay was right—he didn't give a fuck about my wants. That thought made a pain shoot through my heart as a single tear ran down my face. I scooted down on my pillow as more tears followed.

Adonis

Pushing 90 down 495-South heading to my house in Clinton, Maryland, I looked at all the missed calls from Venus and couldn't believe that I forgot about her meeting today. She'd been busting her ass trying to find a company to produce her prototype, and she'd finally found one that was willing to meet with her to discuss her views and ideas. The meeting was scheduled for 5 pm and I was supposed to be home at 4 pm to get our daughter Harmony. This was important for her, and once again I fucked up. I would have been home had I realized that I'd left my phone in the car earlier, because I would have at least received her phone calls. I knew she was pissed and there was no way I could explain to her that I was with Lavelle at Escapes, his new strip club, and her meeting had slipped my mind—especially since she reminded me over and over again this morning.

"SHIT!" I shouted as I slammed my hand against the steering wheel. I tossed the phone on the passenger seat and it immediately started ringing. I hit the answer button on my dashboard and Lavelle's voice came blurring through the speakers.

"Damn nigga, you couldn't come tell me you were leaving?" he asked.

"Shit, yo ass was closed up in the fuckin' office; I thought you was handling yo business, my bad."

"How you like my shit?" he asked with excitement in his voice.

"Yo, that shit is classy as hell, like one of those joints you see them taking Japanese businessmen to in movies and shit, and the bitches? They the fuckin' baddest. I got a lap dance from that bitch Vixen; bitch had a nigga dick hard as fuck," I said. Lavelle burst out laughing.

"Well take yo ass home and let Venus work that nut out," he chuckled.

That was my plan until I saw those missed calls and realized I'd forgotten about her meeting, but I wasn't gonna tell him that. I already knew I had to hear her mouth; I didn't need to hear another one of his damn lectures. He was the only father figure in my life, so he felt that it was his responsibility to teach me how to be a man.

* * * * * * *

When Lavar Thompson, our punk ass daddy, walked out on us, Lavelle became the man of the house. He stepped up and held us down, doing everything in his power to make sure we were straight. At only 15 years old, he had no way of bringing in the type of money Moms needed for all of us to survive, so he turned to hustling. He started off small time, slanging little ass nickel and dime bags of weed to get by, but it still wasn't enough. He had to grind harder and he knew it. He would be out day and night; sometimes we didn't see him for days, but when we did he always had a stack of money for me and momma. She knew what he was doing to get it but looked the other way because it was the only way we could survive without daddy. For years, I watched my brother's grind, and admired his hustle. Most niggas would have gotten cake and tricked it off, but Lavelle was smart. He stacked his money and took care of the family. The known drug dealer peeped his hustle too. Soon, Lavelle went from a local street hustla to the man standing next to the head nigga in charge, Frank Lewis.

Frank owned this city; he had every cop in the neighborhood on his payroll. They even knew about the illegal prostitution in several of his strip clubs, but Frank didn't give a damn. He had one goal in mind: making that bread rise and to the streets, he was the muthafuckin' baker. After going through several right-hand men, Frank found that Lavelle was the most loyal and trustworthy, and gave him the title. By the time Lavelle was 18, he was bringing home more money in a month than Moms made in a year at her nursing job. He knew it was time to get us out of the fuckin' hood. He moved us from our two-bedroom, raggedy ass crib in Barry Farm to a three-bedroom townhouse on Talmadge Circle in Camp Spring, Maryland. Life was good for the Thompsons—for all of us, and Lavelle made sure of that.

Age 16 was the year I officially started feeling myself. Lavelle kept me in fly ass clothes and got me a dope ass whip. A brand new, all-black Ford Explorer was all I ever wanted. I wanted dark tint on the windows with the custom rims on it, but Lavelle was smart and didn't want me to be too flashy. He got me the truck, put light tint on the windows, and told me I had to wait on the custom rims. It was cool 'cause I knew he was only doing what was best for me, and I was grateful he even got me the truck. I sold weed to keep gas in my truck and a little money in my pockets. Lavelle didn't allow me to do too much or sell anything heavy. He really didn't want me in this street life. I had my regulars, and most of them bought the same thing every week. I sold nothing less than a quarter pound; I wasn't wasting my time with nickel and dime bags. I had that good shit that would stink up the place as soon as you opened the bag. I was making good money and got rid of my shit quick. Lavelle was pleased with the way I conducted business and let me handle

all the local customers while he dealt with the hard shit.
Cocaine, heroin, PCP—you name it and he could get it.
Together, we had blocks on lock. Wasn't nobody pushing shit
that wasn't coming through us.

Lavelle taught me everything I knew about the drug game and life in general. I had nothing but love and the upmost respect for him. He valued life and the importance of family; family was above all. He believed in keeping the street shit in the streets and home life separate, and I still lived by that but I could admit that lately, I'd been slipping in my home life. I'd been fuckin' up big time. If Lavelle knew how I'd been slacking, he would hang his foot in my ass, real fuckin' talk. Honestly, Venus and Harmony were my life and I would do anything for them. That's why I was fucked up with myself for not coming through for her today. After seeing a lot of shit niggas went through fuckin' with these bitches out here, I promised myself to never let a bitch get that close to me, but I soon learned that life could change a nigga's mind real quick. I started thinking about the day I met Venus; it was the day that Lavelle gave me my first gun. That day changed me and my life forever.

* * * * * * *

I had just finished serving Jay, one of my regulars, and had to make one last sell to this nigga named Tk. I pulled into the parking lot, then headed up the courtyard toward his apartment building when this hoe named Kim and two of her hoe ass friends walked up on me. Kim had been trying to give me the pussy for a minute, but I was never interested in a bitch that had fucked and sucked every nigga in the hood with a nice whip. Shit, probably the whole damn D.C. area had fucked shorty. I ain't gon' lie, the bitch was bad as fuck and if you ain't know her, then you might fuck up and wife the bitch. To these niggas, Kim was the shit; a short red-bone with big ass titties and a juicy fat ass. For a 16-year-old, she had the body of a grown ass woman. Still, that wasn't enough to get my attention. Shit, I saw bitches with bodies like hers on a daily. I still spoke to her and them other bitches for a quick second, then I made my way to Tk's building. I walked up the stairs and Tk was chilling in the hallway; he gave me dap when I walked over to him. We did our exchange as usual; he pulled out the money first and then I gave him his shit. Just when I was about to turn and leave, this nigga started chatting and shit. That made me feel some type of way 'cause I never talked to this nigga other than giving him the merch, and I had a strange feeling in my gut. This weed head usually never said more than "what's up" and now this muthafucka was running his mouth about some shit I could give two fucks about. I made an excuse and got the hell up out of there. Lavelle always told me if shit didn't feel right, then bounce. I quickly left the building and started walking through the courtyard and from out of nowhere, some niggas jumped me. I didn't see them muthafuckas coming. They all rushed me and I fell on the ground. They started kicking me in the face and throwing blows to my body. I started fighting back and hit one nigga in the jaw and got him up off of me, but then I heard a gun cock and stopped.

"Naw son, you don't want this work," said the big nigga pointing a pistol in my face. Now, I wasn't no bitch ass nigga, but one thing I was taught was that if a nigga points a gun at you, you betta believe he gonna use it. A hundred and fifty dollars wasn't worth my life. The other two flunkies started going through my pockets tryna get whatever they could. Of course, they got nothing. The big nigga kicked me one last time in the face and they hauled ass, but not before they took my brand new pair of Jordans.

"Stupid muthafuckas," I said, getting up and brushing off the dirt. I laughed to myself 'cause them niggas didn't know what they had done, and they had no clue what was coming for them.

I walked down the block to my car, barefoot and embarrassed. I couldn't believe that I let this shit happen to me and I was coming back home with no money or merch. I must have been going 100 mph as I drove back to Lavelle's crib, replaying this shit in my head. How the fuck did I just get jacked by some clown ass niggas? But more importantly, how was my brother going to react when he saw me?

"What the fuck happened to you?" Lavelle asked, hopping off the sofa quick as shit. I didn't even get in the door good and he was already on my ass. I sat on the sofa and ran down the details. I shifted a little and pain shot through my body.

"You good?" Lavelle asked, noting the look of pain on my face.

"Yeah I'm good, just feel a lil' sore." I said as I laid my head on the back of the sofa. He got up and got some ice, and put it on my swollen eye.

"Don't worry, the streets talk. We'll find out who's involved and handle our business. Niggas is grimy and dumb muthafuckas run their mouth, trust me," he shook his head. "You have to show these niggas you ain't to be fucked with, and you ain't playing with their ass. It's a lot of bitch ass niggas gunnin' for you. You can't let nobody get away with shit." he continued.

He reached under the sofa and pulled out a stainless steel case. He sat it on the table and opened it. Inside was a brushed chrome and black 380. He took it out of the case and handed to me. I took it from him and right before leaving, he told me that I need to keep the gun on me on at all times. I sat up on the sofa, admiring the beauty of the gun. This was the first time I had ever held a gun. I saw a bunch of them, but I was holding my own gun in my hands. I took the clip out the gun and aimed it at the wall. I felt powerful and strong, like nobody could stop me as long as I was holding it.

I smiled and said, "On God, ain't nobody takin' shit from me again." then I pulled the trigger. From the rush it gave me, I couldn't wait to do it again but the next time I did it, I was gonna make sure I killed a muthafucka.

* * * * * * *

That was one promise I made to myself that I was able to keep. The other promise I made went out of the fuckin' window as soon as I walked in the store later that evening. I saw Mr. Li struggling with this girl who was tryna steal. She was fine as hell. The first thing I noticed was her oval-shaped, amber-colored eyes that sparkled in the light. She was a caramel complexion with long, naturally curly hair. She had nice sized hips and a plump, round apple ass that was a perfect fit for her small frame, but it was her feisty ass attitude that had my interest; I loved feisty woman. I handled Mr. Li for her, paid for her things, then offered her a ride home. I asked her name and she said that her name was Venus. After that day, we were inseparable. She was the only woman, other than my mother, that was able to get close to me. She completely changed my views about being in love. She captured my heart and had held onto it ever since, but lately I'd been letting her down a lot. When she became 16 and pregnant with Harmony, I had to up my game. Lavelle allowed me to take over some of the traps to make more money in order to properly provide for her and the baby. Since then, I was able to form my own team of runners and had been able to move a lot more product, which added more responsibilities along with way more money. I had been grinding my ass off. I upgraded my whip, my closet, my money, and most of all my lifestyle. I drove a Range Rover, she drove a Benz GL class SUV, and we lived in a four-bedroom, three and a half bath house on Student Drive in Clinton, Maryland. Life was definitely sweet for us but even with all that I had, I still wanted more. I wanted my family to be well off and never want for shit. I never wanted any of my children to experience the shit that me and Venus experienced growing up.

It was a little after 2 am when I pulled into my driveway. I pulled into the garage and turned the ignition off. I sat in the car for a few minutes more trying to think of a valid explanation as to why I didn't make it home on time. I took a deep breath before turning the key and opening the door. I closed the door and locked it, then I placed my keys on the table in the foyer. I noticed that the house was dark. I flipped the light switch on expecting to see Venus sitting on the sofa fuming and ready for a fight. To my surprise, she wasn't. I went in the kitchen and noticed the food storage containers sitting on the stove. Guilt shot through my body, causing me to shake my head in disappointment. This woman even made sure that I had a full course meal waiting for me when I got home and my ass couldn't even leave the fuckin' strip club to be here for her. I placed the containers in the fridge. There was a half-empty bottle of Moët sitting on the shelf, which meant Kay Kay was here giving Venus an ear full. I finished the bottle of Mo and headed upstairs.

I slowly opened the door to Harmony's room and walked over to her bed. Harmony was my spitting image. She had my smooth, dark skin, jet-black hair, and chestnut eyes, but her eyes were oval-shaped like her mother's. I stroked her hair and kissed her forehead. She shifted a little.

"Hi Daddy." she spoke. Her groggy little voice sent light flutters to my heart and made me smile. That little girl lit up even my darkest days.

"Hi, Daddy's baby." I replied as I kneeled beside her and stroked her hair again. "How was your day?" I asked.

"It was good, how was your day?" she asked, stroking my cheek with her tiny little hand. I grabbed her hand from my cheek and kissed it.

"Better now that I see yo pretty little face." I slid my finger gently down her pudgy little nose then kissed the tip of it. "Go back to bed baby." I said, then kissed her forehead again. She nodded, then closed her eyes.

I could hear the TV blaring as I walked down the hallway to our bedroom. I knew Venus was wide awake 'cause she never slept with the TV on. I stood in the hallway for a few minutes preparing for battle, then I walked into the room. She was knocked the fuck out with her laptop on her stomach and sketchpad beside her. I walked over to the bed, removed the laptop and sketchpad, and placed them on the table beside her. I brushed her soft, curly hair from her face, then gently planted a soft kiss on her heart-shaped lips. She didn't move.

I went to the bathroom to take a shower. As I was showering, I thought about how peaceful she looked sleeping. I really didn't want to wake her, but that lap dance mixed with liquor had a nigga horny as hell and I wanted some pussy like right now.

I stepped in the bedroom wearing nothing but a towel. Venus was still asleep on her back with the covers off of one of her legs that was slightly open. My dick instantly got hard. I slid the rest of the comforter off and opened her legs a little wider so that I could slide my tongue in her fat juicy box. She started squirming as I started circling her pearl with my tongue. I felt her closing her legs a little so I started sucking on her pearl. She let out a loud moan and started grinding. She reached down and tried to lift my head, but I sucked a little harder, making her moan even louder. Her sexy ass moans had a nigga's dick throbbing and I was ready to take what was mine, but I wasn't finished feasting on her sweet juices. She slid up trying to break free of me and I wrapped my arms around her thighs, and lifted them up. I grabbed her waist and pulled her back down. I was hungry and she wasn't going no fuckin' where. I started licking from her pearl to her asshole, flicking my tongue in and out of both holes. She started panting like a dog in heat as I devoured her. Her trembling legs let me know that she was about to cream all in my mouth. Still holding on to her legs, I stuck two fingers inside her and started massaging her g-spot while sucking on her clit. Her body started jerking and she let out a long, loud moan as I sucked up all her cum. I climbed on top of her, ready to invade her box with my long thick wood. She placed both hands on my chest and pushed me back.

"Wait, don't think you gon' bring yo ass in this house thinking you gon' get some pussy when you couldn't bring yo ass in here so I could make my meeting. Get the fuck off me."

"What!"

Venus

"What, nigga you heard what the fuck I said. Get...the...fuck...off...me." I said loud and clear as I pushed him up. He really had shit twisted if he thought shit was gon' be that muthafuckin' easy. He had me fucked all the way up.

"I'm sorry." he whispered as he leaned down to kiss me. I put my hand over his mouth to stop him.

"I don't wanna hear that shit, you knew what I had to do. Where the fuck was you?" I asked with a mug on my face. I was mad as hell.

"Vee, I said I'm sorry, damn." he said with a slight attitude, laying on top of me and kissing my neck. I couldn't believe this mothafucka was tryna give me attitude because he wanted to fuck.

"Sorry isn't gon' work this time." I stated, trying to push him up again. He was too fucking strong and it took every little bit of strength in me to try to push him, but his big, tall, strong ass wouldn't budge.

He started sucking on my neck and my body betrayed me. Tingling sensations ran through my body and were gathering in my pearl like I was calling a church meeting or something. Adonis started circling my nipple between his finger and thumb. The satin fabric from my gown had my nipples instantly hard, which only heightened the tingles in my pearl. My eyes started rolling in my head as my body started giving in to his demand.

Fuck it! Fuck now, argue later, I thought as I took his bottom lip in my mouth and let my tongue fill his mouth. If he wanted to do this, then I was gonna remind his ass that I knew his body just like he knew mine, and then I would show him what his ass would miss if I ever did leave him.

I slid my hands down his chest, making sure to trace the outline of his muscular physique, and I continued until I had his shaft in my hand. I started stroking it and playing with my clit with the head of it. He started moaning as he continued sucking my breast.

"You like that?" I whispered in his ear as I ground my clit up and down the tip of his dick, still stroking it at the same time.

"Ummm hmmm." he answered in a low husky moan. I continued doing that until he felt like he was gonna bust all on my box. I placed the tip of his wood at the entrance of my sweetness to feel my wetness.

I turned him over and climbed on top of him. I placed my hands on his chest to support myself as I slowly eased all ten inches inside. I slid up and down his pole slowly so that I could adjust to his size, then I sped up the pace. Looking in his eyes, I fucked him like it was the last time I would ever get that dick. I used my Kegels to tighten the grip around his thick pole as I slid all the way up so that only the head was inside. I started using short, quick strokes to only get the tip inside, teasing him just a little. He grabbed my waist and slammed me down so that he could take control. I pinned his hands behind his head. I wanted him to know that I was in full control. I didn't move. I sat on top of his pole and worked my Kegels, making it feel like I was moving. This nigga started breathing heavy and grinding, trying to get me to actually move, but I tightened my thighs at his waist and started working my Kegels faster, still looking into his eyes. He was moaning just as loud as he had me moaning, his eyes were rolling in his head, and his toes were curling. I just sat there and let my Kegels work the shit out of him. I could feel him at the point of cumin'. I started grinding in circles until I got my nut out, and just as he was about to bust, I slid off of his pole and just sat on top of him.

"Fuck is you doing, fuck you stop for?" he asked with a frowned up face. I started cracking up laughing. He looked at me all puzzled, like I was crazy and shit.

"Nigga, where the fuck was you at?" I gave him the same frowned up face he was giving me.

"What the fuck you mean where I was at? Man, this ain't the time for this muthafuckin' shit. Man fuck that, you always wanna argue about some little shit. You petty as fuck."

"Naw nigga, this ain't about shit being little or petty, it's about where the fuck was you at?" I folded my arms across my chest, giving him an accusatory look. He didn't say a word.

"I'm getting tired of this shit," I spat as I got off of him and stormed to the bathroom.

"Then do something about it." he shouted behind me, stopping me in my tracks.

"What the fuck you just say?" I asked. I turned around so damn quick it felt like I was about to snap my own damn neck. I had my hand on my hip and a scowl on my face waiting for his response.

"Man, you heard what the fuck I said; you tired, then leave. That's what you wanna do? Fine, do it and get the fuck on." he stated with a shrug.

"Really, Adonis?" I gave him a questioning look. He shrugged his shoulders.

"Is that what YOU want? I mean, this isn't the first time you said that shit to me, so if that's what you want then say it. Don't try to turn that shit on me. If it ain't what you want, then make this the last time you say that shit because next time you say it, I will pack me and my daughter's shit up and *get the fuck on*. Trust, that nigga." I pushed his head hard, then started getting my things to take a shower.

"So I can't get a nut?" he asked nonchalantly.

"You got a hand, fuck yourself." I spat before slamming the bathroom door.

After showering, I crawled in the bed, making sure to turn my back on Adonis. He put his arm around me, but I kindly moved it off of me and placed it at his side.

"So I can't hold you?" he asked.

"Not until you tell me what the hell kept you from coming home like you said." I replied.

He let out a sigh and said "I was with Lavelle at his club."

Adonis

"A FUCKIN' STRIP CLUB, ADONIS? I WAS WORRIED, CALLING HOSPITALS AND POLICE STATIONS AND SHIT LOOKING FO YO ASS, AND YOU AT A DAMN STRIP CLUB?" She blew all the way the fuck up. She hopped up so fast, nose flared and eyes all squinted and shit. I swear if looks could kill, a nigga would be dead as fuck right now.

"I'm sorry, Venus. I only stopped through 'cause he just opened. I was 'posed to drop by just to check it out but we started chillin'. I didn't realize I left my phone in the car." I explained.

"I don't give a fuck. You knew since last week what I had to do, and I reminded you this morning so it's no fuckin' excuse why you didn't come home; and on top of that, you didn't drag yo sorry ass in the house until two in the morning. I can't believe this bullshit; you jeopardize me getting a potential business deal for a fuckin' lap dance."

"How you know I got a lap dance?" he asked.

"'CAUSE I KNOW YOU!" she shouted before she exhaled. "This is so fucked up, Adonis. I would never have done anything like that to you."

Her voice was small and brittle, as if she was about to cry. I rubbed my hands down my face and across my beard. I felt like shit. I brushed a string of curls away from her face so that I could look into her amber eyes. I wanted her to see the seriousness in mine.

"I didn't mean to not be there for you. I love you more than anything and I never want to hurt you."

"You did." she stated with a cracked voice and tear-filled eyes.

"I am so sorry; this won't happen again." I grabbed the back of her neck and pulled her in for a kiss. She put her finger over my mouth to stop me.

"You right, it won't happen again 'cause I'm getting a sitter." She laid down with her back turned. There was no need for me to protest; she was gon' hire somebody whether I liked it or not.

The next afternoon, I was awakened by the sweet joyful sounds of my daughter's laughter. I yawned and stretched before getting out of bed. I went to the bathroom, relieved myself, then took care of my hygiene. I had to get rid of the stale alcohol taste that was lingering from last night's drinks. I went in the drawer and got a pair of basketball shorts and a beater and put them on. I walked down the hallway toward Harmony's room. Her giggling and snorting through her nose adorably rippled through the silent hall and bounced off the walls. I felt my love for her fill my heart as I found myself snickering all of sudden. Tears gathered in the corners of my eyes and I wiped them away, then I heard Venus giggling the same snorting giggle as Harmony and I started grinning. I loved my family more than anything in this world, and hearing them laugh filled me with so much joy. I thanked God that they were mine.

"Daaaaddddyy!" Harmony giggled, noticing me stand in the doorway with my arms folded watching her and Venus attack each other with tickles.

"Hey, sweet pea." I beamed. She hopped off of her bed and ran over to me. I picked her up and kissed her all over her face. She started chuckling, tryna get away from my kisses, then I spoke to Venus. She didn't respond. She was obviously still upset with me. I put Harmony down on the bed and kneeled down in front of Venus, taking her hand in mine. I had an apology speech already prepared but when I looked into her eyes, I forgot it and spoke from the heart.

"I know I let you down yesterday. I should have been there for you like you always there for me. I was wrong and it's no excuse. I'm sorry for real baby, and I promise that I will do better. Can you forgive me?" I apologized with a pleading look. She smiled and planted a soft kiss on my lips before accepting my apology. I stood her up and pulled her into my arms. This woman meant the world to me and I loved her to death, on everything.

Harmony came over and hugged my leg. I picked her up and placed her in between me and Venus and we both hugged and kissed her, then started tickling her.

"Hey Harmony, let's get Daddy." Venus snickered, then they turn toward me and started tickling me. I fell back on the bed; Harmony jumped on me, then Venus and we all continued tickling each other. Moments like these were priceless and I was enjoying every minute of playing with my two favorite girls until we were all sprawled over Harmony's bed trying to catch our breath.

My vibrating cell phone interrupted the moment. It was business, so I excused myself and went into the hallway to take the call.

"Aye bruh, I need you to go down to Montana. Some shit went down," Lavelle spoke in a stern tone, informing me that something happened at one of our traps and he needed me to go handle the situation.

"Aight I'ma, call Loco and tell him to meet me there." I replied.

"Do that and call me when you find out something."

"Aight." I hung up. Venus came out into the hallway and asked me what happened. I told her that Lavelle needed me to handle something.

"Ok, well you go handle that and me and lil' momma gon' go see my mother," she said. I nodded in agreement and she kissed me. I hurried and hopped in the shower, got dressed and headed to Montana Avenue, calling Loco from the highway.

I arrived at the trap about 20 minutes later; Loco was already there waiting for me with the workers sitting on the floor lined up in a row. I gave him dap, then paced the back and forth for a second looking at the stupid looks on these nigga's faces.

"What the fuck happened?" I asked Hasson, the nigga in charge.

"Man, CJ was about to serve this nigga Rodney and four niggas rushed us. They had guns on us and shit; one of them muthafuckas hit me with a gun." he explained with a dragging voice, pointing at the cut on his head. I didn't give a fuck about that; I was interested in how much money was lost.

"What they get?" I asked.

"Everything." he replied with a shrug.

"FUCK!" I shouted. I rubbed my hands over my head. My stress level went through the fuckin' roof. Lavelle had just supplied that house and that hit cost us damn near a quarter of a million dollars. I know Lavelle was not gonna wanna hear this bull shit.

"Aye, I think it's time to send these muthafuckas a message," Loco said, running his hand up and down the barrel of his gun.

"You, know who these niggas is?" I asked Hasson.

"Ion know, they had on masks and gloves and shit." he replied. This nigga had the dumbest look on his face, making me wanna spazz on his ass.

"Look, I want y'all niggas' ears and noses to the streets at all times. Put the press on Rodney and any other mutherfucker y'all sell to. I want answers, and I want them like yesterday," I told them. "And get this shit cleaned up," I ordered as I walked toward the door.

I had to go see Lavelle and let him know what was up. I told Loco to make sure they got my shit back in order, and holla at the other hittas on the team and let them know what went down and what I needed.

"Aight bet, I'll hit you lata." he said, giving me dap and a brotherly hug.

Loco was my man. We knew each other since we were kids. I knew him from the neighborhood, but it wasn't 'til we were older that we started kickin' it. I knew he was a crazy ass muthafucka and was down for anything, so naturally, when I gathered my team I made sure to call his ass to be one of my hittas. He didn't give a fuck and he would kill yo ass just for sport, but he was a loyal ass nigga and that was why I fucked with him. I left out of the door and headed to Lavelle's club to give him the information.

Lavelle was sitting in his chair with a scowl on his face talking to Officers Wittman and Dumas, two of the policemen who were on Frank's payroll, when I walked in. Frank's traps that Lavelle oversaw was robbed a few days ago and Lavelle had them tryna get information. He was already frustrated with that; now here I was bringing him more bad news.

"WHAT THE FUCK!" Lavelle thundered, looking like he was about to go on a rampage after I let him know what happened. He was stomping around the office like a raging bull.

"Yo, who the fuck is hittin' my shit?" he asked no one in particular.

"Lavelle, we don't know." Officer Dumas responded. He shrugged his shoulders. "We been trying to get information but no one is talking," he added.

"You mean to tell me that you two incompetent assholes can't shake shit up enough to get me some fucking answers?" The room was silent as he stared at them critically. "What the fuck do you muthafuckas get paid for?" He stormed over to his desk, snatched the bottle of Hennessey, and took a gulp. The hit on the traps had Lavelle thinking that somebody was gunnin' for us, tryna take over.

"Bruh, you know niggas ain't gon' talk to no fuckin' cop. I got Loco and the rest my team on it; we will find some shit out." I stated.

"I know you'll handle shit," he avowed as he sat in his chair, took a deep breath, and dismissed everyone. I stayed behind to asked about the deal with Rojas. Juan Rojas, known in the streets simply as Rojas, was head of a Columbian Cartel and a well-known supplier of some major cities like L.A. and New York. His products were home grown and the best quality on the market. Frank wanted to do business with him, and getting the deal meant a lot more money for all of us.

"So what's goin' on with Rojas?" I asked as I sat in the chair across from his desk.

"I got Maurice handling the deal. Frank don't like it but he trusts me, so it's all good," he answered.

"Man, I'm with Frank on that. I don't think Maurice can handle that shit with his soft ass." I chided.

"Yeah, I'm tryna get his ass on my level so he can get that respect from his father," he shook his head. "I told his ass this was his last chance to prove to Frank that he ready, so he betta come through." he continued.

"Well good luck with that." I got up and gave him dap. "I'm out. I'm about to head home and chill 'til I get word from these niggas."

"Aight man, holla at you lata," he said as he gave me a brotherly hug. I hopped in the car and headed home. I wanted to relax a little, then cook for my family so we could all have dinner together when they got home.

Venus

I was just pulling into my mother's driveway when Ilayna, my 16-year-old little sister, came flying out of the house. She couldn't wait for me to turn the car off to get Harmony out of her car seat.

"Damn Layna, let me turn the car off." I chuckled. I took the key out of the ignition and hit the lock on the door. I reached over the seat and unhooked Harmony from her car seat. The door flew open and Layna snatched her out.

"Hey auntie's girl." she spoke in a high-pitched voice.

"Hey Nayna" Harmony said, wrapping her arms around Layna's neck. Layna loved that she still called her Nayna, even though she could now pronounce her L's. I reached in the back and got my purse and the shopping bags that contained the gifts that I'd bought them.

I took my time getting out of the car. It was always hard for me to face the demons I'd been trying to mask for years. In life, you couldn't really choose your family; you were just born into one. Even though I'd forgiven my mom for all of the fucked up shit she'd put me through, it was still so hard walking into her house. It made no difference to me that it was not the same apartment with the pissy ass smelling hallway I grew up in; the memories were still there. The same sick feelings began to rise from the pit of my stomach every time I walked up the walkway. No matter how hard I tried to move past it, my mind kept taking me back to the day my mom tried to sell me off to get a hit from that glass dick she kept in her mouth.

* * * * * * *

"C'mere, sit on Uncle Willy lap and let me holla at cha," Willy beckoned as I walked out of the kitchen. He was the same man that peeked at me one day while I was in the shower. My mother allowed him to come use the bathroom while I was in there. I was 15 at the time and was almost fully developed. His lust-filled eyes scanned my body, sending chills racing down my spine as he slowly licked his lips. My mother was sitting under him smoking some weed, pretending like she didn't hear this pervert talking to me. He rubbed his hand up and down his thighs as sweat rolled down his face. My mother passed him the blunt. He took a pull and started choking.

"You hear what I said, chile?" he asked, as he blew smoke in my direction.

I looked at my mother, waiting for her to say something to this man but she was mute.

"HELL NO, I AIN'T SITTIN' ON YO LAP YOU PERVERTED BASTARD!" I yelled, my voice filled with rage. I couldn't believe my mother allowed this ugly, stinkin', nasty ass man to ask me to sit on his fuckin' lap. I ran to my room and slammed the door. I tried to lock it but my mother pushed it open before I could turn the lock.

"Girl, you don't talk to no grown ass man like that," she grimaced. She sat down on my bed and pulled me down beside her. "Now, yo momma is sick, and the only way I can get my medicine is you be nice to Willy," she continued. I was mad as hell. This fuckin' cracked out bitch was telling me to let this dirty old man fuck me so she could get some free crack.

"Are you crazy? I am not letting that man touch me." I looked at her with hateful eyes as I continued, "And you are not sick, you are a fuckin' crack head. I am not fuckin' for yo crack, that's what you do."

SMACK!!!

She slapped me so hard she left a red handprint on my face. I tried to rub the burn away as tears rolled down my face.

"How could you, Momma?" I cried as the pain went from my face to my heart. My mother never did anything like that to me before. I was heartbroken.

"Baby, you know I didn't mean to hit you, I just can't let you ruin this for me." She stroked my hair and gave me a *loving embrace. I pushed her off of me. I hated her at that moment.*

"I'm gonna go in my room and he gonna come in here; so be nice, you hear me?" she instructed. I nodded yes with intentions of being anything but nice.

"Look at cha lil' sexy self waitin' on Uncle Willy," he smirked, rubbing his hand over his already hard dick. I was disgusted. I could have vomited all over his trifling ass. I was mad, hurt, and nervous all at the same time. I was breathing so hard I could hardly catch my breath, and my body was shaking so much I had to hold onto the dresser to keep my balance. Sweat beads started to form all over my body as my heart started pounding like a bass drum.

Willy walked over to me and tried to kiss me. His sweaty, musty smell overpowered the stale alcohol and weed smell that lingered from his body. His hot, funky ass breath was running down my neck as whispered in my ear.

"You play nice now, you hear?" I grabbed the soda bottle off my dresser and cracked him upside his head.

"You lil' bitch," he retorted with a smack across my face, right in the same place momma smacked me. I grabbed my burning cheek. "We can do this easy or hard, it's up to you," he said as he grabbed me by the throat and squeezed it a little.

"AAUGH!" he cried out after I kicked him in the balls. I tried to run, but he grabbed me by my leg.

"Get the fuck off of me!" I shouted as I tried to kick away from him.

"Ok, you wanna do this the hard way, no fuckin' problem," he snapped, snatching me off of the floor. He threw me on the bed and pinned me down. I was squirming, trying to free myself from his grip. I remembered that I had a knife under my bed. I was moving too much for him to get my clothes off. He let go of my hand and slapped me again.

"I'm gonna have to teach yo lil' ass a real lesson." He held me down by my neck as he started taking off his belt. My heart was racing and I was out of breath from struggling with him. I felt like giving up and letting him do what he wanted, but something inside of me told me to keep fighting. I started bucking like I was riding a bull, trying to get him off of me. He straddled me so that I couldn't move my legs anymore.

"Yeah, I know you want it," he chuckled as he ran his rough hands up my shirt and started squeezing my breast. I never felt so disgusted in my life. I slowly eased my hand down the side of the mattress. I felt the handle of a knife sticking out. I gripped it as tight as I could and eased it from the mattress. I plunged the knife deep into his shoulder and *pulled it back out. He tried reaching for it but I swung it, stabbing him in his arm. He grabbed his arm as the blood started trickling down. I started kicking again, catching him in the nuts again. He fell over on the side of me. I quickly hopped off of the bed, grabbed the phone, and walked backward out of my room. My mother was standing in the hallway with tears in her eyes.*

"What did you do?" she asked, noticing Willy's blood on my shirt. I didn't respond. I ran down the steps as she ran into my room hollering Willy's name. I ran out of the door, still holding the knife. I ran down the street as fast as I could, looking back to make sure he wasn't following me. I was scared and I kept tripping over my feet, stumbling so I wouldn't fall. When I was sure I was far enough from home, I stopped running. My nerves kicked in and I started throwing up. I sat down on the steps trying to calm down. I called Adonis and as soon as he answered, I broke down. The next night, Adonis and Lavelle went looking for Willy's ass and since I didn't want them to kill him, they beat him into a coma. We never heard from nasty ass Willy again. Me and my mother never spoke about my childhood or that dreadful night, and I sometimes wondered if it was a conversation worth having. It wasn't easy to move forward, but we both put in effort and had made tremendous progress. We actually

had that mother and daughter relationship I longed for growing up. I guess some things were better left unsaid.

* * * * * * *

"VEE, VENUS!" Layna shouting my name snapped me out of my memory.

"You coming? What's wrong with you?" she questioned, confused and wondering why I was still sitting in the car.

"I'm coming." I replied. I let out a deep breath, smiled, and got out of the car.

Layna held the door open for me since my hands were full. I walked in the living and sat the bags down beside the chair. My mother was sitting on the sofa watching TV with Daquan, my 17-year-old brother, and she smiled at me. Seeing her beautiful smile and knowing that she was still sober surpassed the pain that I kept buried deep in my heart.

"Aye, what's up sis." Daquan said as he gave me a head nod. I walked over to my mother, gave her a hug and kiss, and asked how was she doing.

"I'm doing good, how are you doing?" she asked. I flopped down in the chair and shrugged my shoulders.

"What's going on?" she asked with a look of concern. I told her that we would talk in private a little later, then I reached in the bag and gave her the Louis Vuitton purse and Coach sneakers I bought her. She thanked me and gave me another hug.

"NO YOU DIDN'T!" Layna shouted when I passed her the Gucci purse that she wanted. I giggled at her excitement.

"Where my gift at?" Daquan asked, noting the gifts I gave my mother and sister.

"Boy, you ain't got no gift." I said, sitting back in the chair crossing my legs. He had a look of disappointment on his face and I almost burst out laughing.

"Boy here." I said, passing him a bag. He opened it and pulled out the Giuseppes I got him.

"Oh, thanks sis. These the ones I liked too." he beamed, grinning from ear to ear. I watched the excitement on my family's faces as they admired their gifts. Being able to provide my family with things that I never thought I could possibly have myself made me love Adonis more. If it wasn't for him, I wouldn't be able to do these things for them. That's why I was confused about what to do about the relationship.

My mother asked Layna and Quan to take Harmony upstairs so that we could talk. As soon as they were out of sight, she turned toward me and placed her hands over top of mine.

"Ok now tell me, what's going on?" she asked in a softly spoken voice.

"I don't know, Ma. I just feel like Adonis is changing. Like he really don't care about me anymore." I spoke truthfully.

"Listen girl, relationships have ups and downs. You just have to do whatever you have to do to get through the bad times," she advised. "Besides, Adonis is a good man. Look at all he's done for you—shit, for this family, starting with putting me in that nice rehab place. If it wasn't for him, who knows where I would be. Not living in no three-bedroom townhouse, that's for sure, especially in a nice neighborhood like this." she continued.

Adonis got her this house after she completed rehab. He wanted her and my siblings to start fresh in a nice area. He didn't want me to worry about them so much. Adonis was a good man and I appreciated all that he'd done for me and my family, but I couldn't ignore what I was feeling inside. I couldn't ignore the fact that he made me feel unimportant.

"Ma, I understand what he's done and I am so grateful, but I can't go on feeling the way I do. I want more out of life for myself, and he makes me feel like what I want is not important." I explained.

"Well look, sometimes in a relationship, you have to sacrifice your own wants and needs to keep your man happy." She stated. I had no clue what the hell she was talking about. What about my happiness? I had sacrificed my wants and needs long enough and if Adonis couldn't support me on that, then I would have to do what I had to do.

"You right, Ma." I agreed, only because there was no use in talking to her about it anymore. She idolized Adonis and he couldn't do no wrong in her eyes. I could tell her that he beat and cheated on me, and she would still find a way to tell me what I needed to do to please him.

A couple hours later, I getting ready to leave and Layna asked if Harmony could stay with her for the night. I needed to get some work done anyway so I let her stay. I gave my mother some money for herself and money for Harmony, then grabbed her monthly bills and headed home. Driving down the highway, I wondered about my relationship. I wondered if what I was feeling was real, or if those feelings were coming from something deep within my own mind.

I opened the door to my house and the smell of food cooking invaded my nostrils, causing my stomach to growl. I slowly walked down the foyer, surprised that Adonis was home so early, but I was mostly surprised that he had the house cleaned and was cooking dinner. I stepped into the living room and he was standing there wearing some dark blue Ferragamo pants and a button up, surrounded by the flickering of candles and looking sexy as ever. I loved how the pants showed off his slight bow legs, and the cream-colored Christian Louboutin Pik boat shoes added that extra flare to the outfit. He was holding a bouquet of long stem roses. He walked over to me with the biggest smile on his face, reminding me how genuinely thoughtful he really was.

"Welcome home baby." he said, in a smoky tone. He passed me the flowers, then planted a quick peck on my lips. He took my purse and keys, placed them on the table, then took my hand.

"Adonis what is this?" I asked, still shocked.

"This is my way of formally apologizing to you, and showing you that I'm gon' do better," he stated. He kissed my hand and led me to the dining room, which was lit up by candles. There were two stick candles in their holders in the center, with tea light candles around them in a shape of a heart and rose petals covering the top of the table. On the corner was a bucket of ice wrapped in a red covering containing a bottle of wine. The table was already set with all the tableware, including wine glasses

"Adonis this is breathtaking." I complimented as he pulled out the chair for me to sit. I sat down and he pushed my chair under.

"I'll be right back." he brushed the hair from my face and cupped my chin in his hand.

"I love you." he said in a sexy low voice. He kissed me passionately, then disappeared into the kitchen.

He came back with a tray containing our meal—Maine lobster tails stuffed with crabmeat and shrimp, two six-ounce filet mignon steaks, two bowls of New England clam chowder and two crab cakes. I was in awe. I couldn't take my eyes off of him as he placed the trays on the table and served our food.

"I haven't seen that smile in a while." he said as he filled our wine glasses. I was smiling so hard that my cheeks started to hurt.

"I'm just so speechless right now." I replied. He smirked with a little snicker.

"Wait until you see what's next." He said, then kissed me.

After dinner, he led me upstairs to our bedroom and told me to get undressed. He went into the bathroom and turned on the water in the tub. He came out of the bathroom nude. He placed his hands over my eyes and walked me into the bathroom. He removed his hands and I opened my eyes. I was in awe looking at the sight. The bathroom was decorated even more beautifully than the dining room. The scent of the milk and honey bubble bath that I loved filled the air as candles surrounded the tub. Rose petals made a trail from the door to the inside of the tub. The rose petals floated beautifully against the milky white water. On the side of the tub was a small tray holding another bottle of wine, two wine glasses, and a tray of cheesecake-filled strawberries dipped in chocolate. He stepped in the tub first, then took my hand and helped me step in with him. The warm water relaxed me; he pulled me closer and laid my head against his chest, then he picked up a strawberry and fed me.

"I see you didn't ask why Harmony's not here." I stated as I took another bite out of the juicy strawberry. I dripped a little of the filling on my chest. Adonis scooped it off with his finger, then sucked it off before responding.

"I called Layna and asked for a favor. I wanted you all to myself tonight," he replied. He moved my hair to the side and gently sucked then bit my neck, causing my body to quiver. After the bath, he rubbed me down with oil.

"Do you forgive me?" he whispered as he gently sucked my ear lobe into his mouth.

"All is forgiven." I replied as he pulled me closer into his arms and kissed me passionately, then we made love. It was on a level of intimacy that we had never reached. We took our time exploring each other's bodies in ways that we'd never explored each other before. That night, all the fears I had about our relationship disappeared. I mattered, and he made me feel like I was important.

Adonis

"Good morning baby." Venus simpered, waking me up by climbing on top of me and preparing to ride me. I was still tired from the all-nighter we pulled the night before but fuck that, I wasn't ever gonna turn down waking up to some pussy.

"Good morning." I replied, grabbing by the back of her neck and pulling her down for a kiss. I grabbed her by the waist so that I could plunge deeper inside of her already dripping wet box. She gasped loudly. She placed her hand on my chest for balance as she bounced up and down on my dick. Her muscle tightened around my shaft and I held her down by her shoulders, thrusting roughly inside her.

"Shit Adonis." She breathed with her eyes closed. I continued my stroke, pounding deeper every time she came down on me. My phone started ringing, interrupting the sex. I ignored it. As soon as we started again, the phone started ringing it again.

"Answer it." She breathed with frustration in her tone.

"Fuck no, I'm busy," I replied, still keeping my stroke. I wasn't about to stop handling my business to answer no damn phone. It started ringing for the third time.

"FUCK!" I shouted as I reached for the phone. As soon as I answered, we both exploded. She laid down on my chest.

"Yeah." I breathed into the phone with an attitude.

"Nigga, get the fuck outta the pussy." Loco laughed loud as fuck into the phone. I don't give a fuck what time it was, that muthafucka was always on a thousand.

"Man, calm yo loud ass down and tell me what the fuck you on my line for this muthafuckin' early." I demanded.

"We got information, you pussy whipped muthafucka." he marveled. That got my ass up.

"Say less, I'll see you in an hour at Escapades." I commanded. I jumped out of bed and rushed in the shower. I threw on my clothes and zoomed out the door.

Loco was sitting on the sofa watching the strippers on the monitor when I walked in Lavelle's office. I shook my head as I walked over to him.

"STOP LOOKIN AT THEM BITCHES!" I yelled in his ear, startling him.

"Nigga fuck that, they fat as fuck." he pointed out as he turned back toward the monitor.

"You here on business, remember that." Lavelle blurted from behind his desk.

I walked over to him and gave him a brotherly hug. I sat down on the edge of his desk.

"Loco, get your mind off them bitches and tell me what you found out." I commanded.

He turned around and told us that this nigga named Slick was one of the guys that robbed our trap. Slick was known around the hood for jackin' muthafuckas and I guess he thought that it would be cool to run up in our shit, but he would soon find out that we didn't take that shit lightly.

"So what's the plan?" Lavelle asked.

"I say we hit the nigga at his crib," Loco suggested. I agreed, and so did Lavelle. "I got eyes on him, we can ride out tonight if you want." he added.

"Shit, I'm down," I said. Lavelle told us to take Smoke, one of his hittas, with us. I made a quick call to Dirty, a driver, and told him where to meet us and what time, then Loco and I came up with a plan to run up in Slick's spot unnoticed.

Later that night, me, Loco, Smoke, and Dirty got suited and dressed in all black everything. We hopped in Dirty's car and headed to Slick's house.

"So everybody know the plan, right? Y'all ready?" I asked Loco and Smoke as we pulled behind the dumpster in the parking lot next to his house.

"Hell yea, you know I stay ready." Loco sneered. "You know me, I'm always down to murda a nigga," he continued.

"This muthafucka always get excited when it's time to put in work." Dirty laughed, pointing back at Loco.

"Shit nigga, that's the only way to be." Loco replied.

"Aight, you know the drill. Keep the lights out and the car runnin'." I told Dirty as we put our gloves and mask on.

Loco crept up to the house and peeked in all the windows. He gave a signal telling us that it was clear. We started creeping up to the house. I was laughing like shit on the inside watching Smoke's big tall Debo-looking ass tryna crouch down and run at the same time. Loco had already climbed through a window and was in the house when we made it to the back door. He opened the door.

"AAAAAHHHH, YEEEES BABY!" Loud sex noises filled the hall as we slowly crept up the steps, careful not to make any noise. Loco looked at me and shook his head.

"Too bad that's the last piece of pussy his ass ever gonna get." he mouthed. I gave him a humorless look that made him get serious.

The bed hitting the wall masked the sound of the steps creaking under our feet as we made our way to the top.

Loco stood at the front of the bedroom door, anxious to kick the bitch in. I gave him the signal.

BOOM!

He kicked the door in.

"GET THE FUCK ON THE GROUND!" he shouted, pointing the gun at the couple. Slick tried to jump up quickly and fell on the floor.

The girl started screaming.

"SHUT THE FUCK UP BEFORE I CUT YO FUCKIN' TONGUE OUT!" Smoke shouted, then smacked her in the face with his gun.

"W...w...what the fuck is this a...a...about?" Slick asked, stuttering and shit, scared as a muthafucka.

I sat on the side of the bed and ran the gun up and down his bitch's thick, sexy ass thigh. She was curled up in a ball trembling uncontrollably. The rapid rise and fall of her chest let me know that her heart was racing.

"What's your name, sweetheart?" I asked in a soothing tone.

"Sh...Shan....tel." she stuttered as tears formed in her eyes.

"Look baby, ain't nobody gon' hurt you as long as yo nigga give me the answers I want." I stated, as I caressed her cheek with my gun. "See, him and some other muthafuckas robbed a trap, and I want to know who sent him?" I added.

"M...m...man I don't know nothing 'bout no trap." he said with a tremulous voice. It was obvious to me that his bitch ass was lying.

I shook my head and said "Wrong answer."

He was still laying on the ground on his side with Loco's gun pointed at his temple. I stepped on his dick. This nigga started screaming. Smoke covered his mouth with the pillow to silence his scream. I took my foot off of him. He doubled over, trembling in pain and holding his dick. Loco kneeled down in front of him.

"I suggest you tell the truth, 'cause this nigga ain't playin'. He will torture you until you be beggin' me to kill you." he spoke the truth. If we were at the warehouse, I would torture his ass within an inch of his life just for general purpose, but since we weren't I'd have to keep this shit on the low. The nigga still didn't talk.

I started to step on his lil' ass dick again, but Loco's crazy ass was getting antsy and before I could do anything, he said, "Fuck this shit." He beat the shit outta the nigga with the butt of the gun.

Slick laid there crying like a lil' bitch, but he still didn't open his mouth. I thought that it was time to show his ass what was really good. I gave Smoke a signal and he broke this nigga's finger. He screamed in pain. I nodded my head and he broke another one. The sound of his bones breaking made his bitch cringe and cover her ears.

"Tell them, Slick; tell them whatever they wanna know, please." Shantel pleaded as she sobbed. His ass still didn't speak.

Smoke broke two more of the nigga's fingers, then he started singing like a bird. He told us that some nigga paid him and three other niggas that he didn't know ten grand each to hit the houses. He told them when to do it, how to do it, and where the money and merch was kept. Whoever hired him knew the ins and outs of the traps. He told us that he couldn't give us a name because the bitch muthafucker never told them who he was. Everything was done in secret. I looked into his eyes and could tell that he was telling the truth. Loco started pistol whippin' the nigga again, splattering his blood all over the walls. Some even got on his bitch's legs. She looked as if she wanted to scream, but she knew better. Smoke was serious about cutting her tongue out.

"You know street code. You better keep your mouth shut or we will find your ass, and I promise that by the time I finish with you, dental records won't be enough to identify you," I warned. I wiped the blood off of her leg and rubbed it on her trembling lips.

"Take care of yourself." I smirked. I got up and signaled my crew to leave.

As we were walking out the door, I nodded to Loco and he put the pillow over Slick's face and shot him twice in the head. Shantel covered her mouth and started screaming into the pillow as his brain matter splashed all over the side of the bed. Loco walked over to her and removed the pillow from her face. She was visibly shaken. Her body was trembling even more now, her breathing was labored, her eyes were open as wide as they could go, and she was shaking her head no with a pleading look on her face.

"Damn ma, you fine and sexy as fuck. I'ma be back for you, believe that." he said, then blew her a kiss as we walked out the door.

"Loco, you crazy ass muthafucka; why you scare that girl like that?" Smoke asked, laughing as we climbed in the car.

"Man shit, I might have to get at shawty. Her nigga dead now, I know that bitch gonna need some comforting. She just been through some traumatic ass shit." he laughed.

"Nigga, yo mind fucked up," I said, shaking my head.

Even though we got Slick's ass, I was pissed. I still had no answers. I guess that meant we'd have to shake shit up and put fear in these muthafuckas' hearts; let them know I ain't to be fucked with. We drove the car back to the garage to dump everything before parting ways.

"Aye, I'ma come through in a lil' while and chill for a minute." Loco informed me.

"Cool, see you lata." I gave him dap, then headed home to do my normal after-kill routine" shower, fuck, and eat— in that muthafuckin' order.

I walked in the house and Venus and Kay Kay were sitting on the sofa going over some design choices. I spoke and proceeded to go shower. After showering, I called Venus to the room. She came in looking sexy as fuck in her short shorts with no panties and tank top with no bra. I didn't want to disturb her but I needed to take my frustrations out on something, and what better way to do it than to break her fuckin' back? I pulled her over to me and started taking off her clothes. She tried to protest at first, but when she saw the hungry look in my eyes she knew that it was no use fighting the inevitable. I laid her on the bed, parted her legs, and gave her clit a hell of a kiss with my tongue. She started squirming and moaning as I continue to devour her juices like I was dying of thirst; then I flipped her over and used my knee to spread her legs.

"DAMN, ADONIS!" she shouted as I entered her roughly. "You tryna fuck my insides up?" she questioned. I ignored her. I grabbed her by her waist and continued pounding deeper and deeper inside of her, relieving my frustrations with every thrust.

"OOOH   SH   SH   SHIIIIT AAAA...DDDOO...ONN...ISSS   YOU   YOU!"   she sputtered. I was hittin' her so hard that she could hardly form words. I continued my stroke until I exploded inside her. I smacked her hard on her ass leaving a light pink hand print, then laid back on the bed. She slowly got up to go to the bathroom.

"Make sure you put on bra and panties." 'cause Loco coming over," I called behind her.

"Oh shit! I forgot Kay Kay is downstairs." She quickly grabbed her clothes and rushed into the bathroom.

"I can't believe we did this with her downstairs." she fussed as she came out of the bathroom hurrying to put on her clothes. She threw her towel at me, then rushed downstairs.

"Y'all so nasty." I heard Kay Kay chuckle when Venus made it into the living room. I laughed, then got dressed.

I went into the kitchen and warmed up some food, then joined them in the living room. Kay Kay had already put their sketches away and was halfway through a bottle of wine. I sat down and placed my plate on the coffee table.

"Damn nigga, you hungry?" Kay Kay asked, noticing all the food on my plate.

"Starving." I replied with a fork full of food in my mouth.

"I bet." she smirked as she took another sip of wine. The doorbell started ringing. Knowing it was Loco, I took my time answering it.

"Damn nigga, what the fuck took you so fuckin' long to open the damn door?" he sneered as he stepped in the door.

"Shut the fuck up, you lucky I let your rude ass in." I grimaced, closing the door behind him. As we were walking down the foyer, he stopped short.

"Aye man, who the fuck is that?" he asked, pointing at Kay Kay.

"That's Kaylee, Venus' friend." I replied.

"Shit man, I need to come over more often. Introduce a nigga." he said.

I shook my head, "Man come on." I chuckled, motioning him to the living room.

Venus got up and hugged Loco, then introduced him to Kay Kay.

Kay Kay

"Loco, this Kaylee; Kaylee, Loco." Venus introduced. I looked that fine ass nigga up and down before offering him my hand to shake. He was extremely tall, about six feet seven and, about 260 pounds of all muscle. His skin was the color of milk chocolate. His eyes were small, dark, and mysterious, and his sexy ass lips were thick and juicy; I wanted to suck on them. At first glance, he kind of put you in mind of a dark-skinned L.L. Cool J with shoulder-length dreads. I was in love.

"Call me Kay Kay; it's nice to meet you, Loco. So tell me, are you really crazy or is that just a name?" I asked, batting my eyes.

He leaned closer to me "Nah baby, Loco is a name 'cause I'm more than crazy, I'm fuckin' psycho." he smirked, then kissed my hand. "It's nice to meet you too, ma," he added.

His deep, raspy voice vibrated through my ears and ended up in my kitty cat. Everything about this man screamed sex appeal, and he had me wanting to jump on his ass right now. Him and Adonis went into the basement to chill while Venus and I went into the family room to find a movie to watch.

About an hour later, I was standing in the kitchen opening a bottle of wine. My back was turned and I didn't hear anyone come in. Suddenly, I was pinned against the counter from behind.

"That ass is fat, ma." Loco said, his voice smoky as he whispered in my ear and pressed against me. I could feel his bulge pressing against my lower back. His warm breath lightly brushed my neck, sending quivers down my spine. The scent of his Creed cologne was like an aphrodisiac sending sudden warm sensations through my body. I closed my eyes and bit down on my bottom lip as my breathing became shallow.

"I wanna bend yo ass over this counter right now." he breathed. His words sent tingles to my kitty cat and I could feel myself getting moist. He slid his hand up the side of my thighs and wrapped his arms around my waist.

"Look, I'ma leave in a few; I want you to come with me." He sucked my earlobe in his mouth and flicked it with his tongue, causing me to shiver. He turned me around to face him. His gaze held mine as he sucked his bottom lip in his mouth and released it slowly. I swallowed, trying to moisten my dry throat. He gave me a half smile then leaned close to me as if he was going to kiss me. I let out a slow breath. A sudden feeling of light-headedness rushed through me. I had to grip the counter to keep my balance.

"I'm gonna wait for you in the back of the gas station on the corner, 20 minutes tops. If you want me, you will come; if you don't come then I will look at it as a challenge." He licked his lips, then lifted my chin. "I love a good challenge." he stated, then gave me a slightly open-mouthed lingering kiss as he gripped a hand full of my ass.

"MMM MMM MMM, the things I can do to you" he moaned. He gave me one last once-over, then disappeared back into the basement. I let out the breath that I was holding. I grabbed the bottle of wine and took a big gulp out of it. I had never been so turned on in my life.

"What the hell taking you so damn long?" Venus asked, walking in the kitchen. I jumped like I was just caught doing something wrong. I looked at her wide-eyed with guilt written all over my face. She gave me a quizzical look, then placed her hand over her opened mouth.

"You was fuckin' with Loco, wasn't you?" she asked, already knowing the answer. I was at a loss for words.

"Giiiirrrllll," was all she could say as she threw her head back with her hands on the top of her head.

Loco and Adonis came upstairs. I gave Venus a pleading look, hoping she wouldn't say anything and she didn't. Loco gave Venus a hug goodbye. He hugged me and whispered, "Twenty minutes," in my ear, then gave me another half-smile before walking away. My heart was pounding. Venus smirked, shaking her head as Adonis walked Loco to the door. I quickly poured myself another glass of wine and took a gulp. I was trying to decide if I was going to go meet up with Loco or not. My body wanted to know what he could do with that big ass bulge he was poking me with, but my mind was saying, *"Bitch, you don't know this nigga, go your ass home."* I looked at the clock, gulped down the rest of my wine, then told Venus that I would talk to her later and hurried out the door.

I pulled into the back of the gas station; Loco was leaning against his black Ford Expedition with tinted windows and custom chrome rims, drinking a bottle Pepsi and looking sexy as hell. I pulled next to him and got out of the car. He smirked, then motioned me to come here. I leaned against my car with my arms crossed, pretending like I didn't want to run over to him and kiss those luscious lips of his. He crossed his arms over his chest, mimicking my stance. I giggled, then took a few steps toward him. He reached out and grabbed me by my jeans, pulling me closer.

"I knew you would come." He said as he pulled me in for a kiss. He slid his hands down my back and gripped my ass, pulling me deeper into the kiss. Rubbing on his pole, I sucked on his tongue. He let out a guttural moan. I felt him starting to get hard. I started gently biting on his neck, then sucking on it. The lustful look in his eyes let me know that he was turned on and ready to fuck.

"Get in." He demanded, opening his car door. I took a few steps back, putting some distance between us.

"Nah baby, it's not that easy." I said, closing his door.

"Are you serious right now?" he questioned with a confused look on his face.

I tossed my hair to the side and twirled a string around my finger, giving him a look that said *you damn right I'm serious.* He leaned back against his car with his hands folded in a fist and legs crossed at the ankles, looking me up and down while licking his lips.

"So what, you came to give me a little taste?" he asked with a smirk on his face. I got in my car.

"Just a little bit, until I know for sure you can handle the real thing." I giggled, flirting.

He laughed then said, "Aight, you like playing games?"

"I wouldn't call it a game, it's a challenge. You said you love a good challenge, right?" I asked, giving him a questioning look as I batted my eyes. I started my car, then I held my business card out of the window.

"Challenge accepted." he stated as he took the card out of my hand. I blew him a kiss and sped out of the gas station.

Loco

I was cracking up laughing as Kay Kay pulled out of the gas station. She really thought she had a nigga open. Her little so-called tease only made me want to prove a point. I had that life-changing dick and she had no idea what was in store for her. If she knew the things I was capable of, she wouldn't play those types of games. She challenged me; that was funny. The last person who challenged me was six feet deep right now. I shook my head and got in my car.

"I'm gon' murda that pussy." I boasted as I turned the key in the ignition. "The Kay Kay she knows and loves just died. May she rest in peace," I added. I kissed the gold cross that I wore around my neck to remind me that only God could judge me, then pulled out of the gas station.

The wind breezed through my window as I headed down Branch Avenue, heading to my house on D Street in Northeast D.C., thinking about how to get at Kay Kay. She wanted a nigga to chase her, but that wouldn't happen. I didn't chase no bitch; I made them come to me. I turned onto my street and parked in front of my house just as my phone began ringing. It was Adonis.

* * * * * * *

Me and Adonis go way back; I knew him from my childhood neighborhood. Back then, I didn't want anyone gettin' into my business so I stayed to myself. My home life was fucked up. My pops used to beat on my mother and when I tried to defend her, he would beat my ass. He would beat me like I was a random nigga on the streets. I had to stay home from school to hide the black eyes and bruises that he left all over my body. I wouldn't go outside either. Every time I heard my mother screaming, I would become enraged; I felt helpless. I would hide in the closet and cover my ears crying, trying to block out the sounds of my big ass pops, who was 6'8 and 300 pounds, beating on my little 5'5, 145-pound defenseless mother. That went on most of my childhood, but I didn't tell because I didn't want to be taken away from my mother. I couldn't imagine her going through that without me there to protect her, even though I was no help for real for real.

The older I got, the angrier I became. I hated the world, and anyone that came at me sideways got handled real quick. Everyone in the neighborhood knew not to fuck with Orlando Tyrell Gaines, a.k.a Loco. I would stay gettin' suspended from school and I didn't give a fuck about the ass whippin' I would get from my pops behind the suspension. As long as I was able to release the anger I had against my pops on somebody, I was good. That was how I met Adonis.

I was in the cafeteria minding my fuckin' business and this nigga that had a rep for being the toughest in the school and thought he would try me. He came to my table and pulled me up by my collar and shit.

"So you the one they call O, huh?" he asked with a mug on his face. I didn't respond.

"You don't look like you bad; I bet I can beat your ass." he said. I still didn't respond.

He got mad, poking his chest out and shit, tryna flex on a nigga. I burst out laughing. This muthafucka tried to swing on me. I dodge his weak ass punch and caught him with a swift right hook. He fell onto the table and I picked up my lunch tray, beating the shit outta his ass. The lil' nigga was leaking all on the table. Adonis ran over there and I thought he was comin' at me too, so I swung on his ass. He dodged a couple of them but one landed and bust his lip. We were both sent to the principal's office while that other lil' nigga had to go to the hospital. Me and Adonis started talkin' in the lobby of the principal's office and he explained to me that he was tryna break up the fight. We both started laughing about the whole situation. I took all the blame and got expelled for the rest of the year. My pops had a field day beatin' my ass. After that, I would see Adonis around the hood every once in a while; we would speak, but I was still standoffish. My beatings were more severe and since I wasn't in school anymore and didn't have to hide the bruises, he could do whatever he wanted.

That summer, the world came crashin' down on me. My pops got a gun and threatened to kill me and my mother, and I believed him. One day, he came home pissed off over something at work. My mother was in the kitchen cooking. I was sitting at the table talkin' to her. He came raging in the kitchen and without sayin' a word, he punched her in the face so hard that she fell on the floor. I called out to her. He gave me a look letting me know that I was next, then started rainin' blows down on my mother. She was screaming and beggin' him to stop, but her cries fell on deaf ears. I knew I had to do something to help her. I remembered the gun that he kept waving around at us. I ran out of the kitchen into the front closet and got it. I ran back in the kitchen.

"GET OFF MY MOMMA BEFORE I KILL YOU! I shouted. He looked at me and laughed.

"Oh, so you gon' shoot me, yo daddy? Then go ahead, shoot me." he said with outstretched arms. My mother was on the floor beggin' me to put the gun down. My pops gave me an evil look as he began taunting me.

"Look at cha, shakin' like a leaf, scared to death. You ain't gon' do shit, you little punk." he said with a faint, satiric smile. He started coming toward me.

"NO, LEAVE HIM ALONE!" my mother yelled as she grabbed his leg. He tried kicking his leg to release himself from her grip but she had a strong hold on his pant leg.

"IMMA KILL BOTH OF Y'ALL TODAY!" he shouted as he turned around and punched her again. I shot him twice in the back, killing him almost instantly. An overwhelming feeling of peace mixed with satisfaction shot through my body like a bolt of lightning and I felt relieved. I was 11 years old. It wasn't considered self-defense because I wasn't in immediate danger and I shot him in the back. Due to the abuse I suffered, the judge was lenient on me and gave me five years in juvie. When I got out, I ran into Adonis and we'd been kicking ever since. He was the only person I ever told about the shit that was going on in my house.

* * * * * * *

"What's up?" I answered.

"I was just thinking about what we discussed earlier. I think you're right. It's in the house." he replied.

"Now we need to figure out where," I avowed.

"Aight, see you." Adonis hung up and I took my ass in the house, hopped in the shower, and called me a bitch to finish what Kay Kay's fine ass started.

Adonis

It had been a couple of weeks since our traps got hit and we still hadn't found out who the other niggas were. I had been so stressed the fuck out that it started causing problems between me and Venus again. We hadn't really been speaking to each other the past few days. Tonight, I was just angry for no reason and got upset because she complained about me not helping her fold laundry. She and Kay Kay had another meeting with the manufacturing company that was making the prototype for their clothing line, and she'd spent most of her day cleaning, cooking, and taking care of Harmony as well as preparing for her meeting. She asked me to help her fold the two hampers full of laundry that she washed earlier. I was laying back looking at ESPN and didn't feel like folding laundry, so when she asked I exploded.

"DON'T YOU SEE ME WATCHIN' TV?" I snapped. "You wait until I am trying to relax to ask me to do something, fuck. You do this shit all the fuckin' time, and it gets on my damn nerves," I ranted.

"Adonis, I hardly ever to ask you to do any damn thing around this fuckin' house. I am tired, I had a long day, and I want to go to bed. All I'm asking you to do is to help me, damn! Is that too much?" she fussed.

"Yeah, it's too damn much when I been out all day doin' shit to make sure I can pay all the muthafuckin' bills in this fuckin' house. Why the fuck you wanted this house if you didn't want to clean the shit?"

"What fuck are you talkin' about? YOU wanted the house just as much as I did, and YOU wanted me to stay home with Harmony. Now, I am trying to have a career so that I can bring in some money, but thanks for telling me how you really feel." she said. I could see tears forming in her eyes. She looked hurt, but at that moment I didn't care.

"Oh, don't try that *oh my feelings hurt* look with me because I really don't give a fuck right now. You want the fuckin' clothes folded, then fold them and leave me the fuck alone." I spat.

She started to respond but I answered my ringing phone before she could open her mouth. It was Lavelle. He noticed the anger in my voice and knowing how stressed I'd been lately, he suggested that I come over to his house to play Spades with him and his close friends Raymond and Eddie. They had been his boys since our days in Barry Farm. They both sold drugs with him for a little while in high school, but Raymond got a scholarship to Morehouse College in Atlanta, and Eddie married his high school sweetheart and had five kids. They tried to get together once or twice a month to chill, making sure that they don't lose their bond. I agreed to go. I needed to get out of the house before I continued to take my frustrations out on Venus, knowing good and damn well that she didn't deserve it.

"WHAT THE FUCK IS YOU DOIN' NIGGA?" Lavelle miffed. Eddie had reneged on a play.

"Yo ass played a spade on a fuckin' diamond last time. What the fuck was you thinkin?" Lavelle ranted. I was doubled over in my chair, laughin' so hard that my stomach muscles hurt. Lavalle was heated. He thought that he was the muthafuckin' king of spades and that no one could beat him.

"Nigga I fucked up, I had my fuckin' cards mixed up." Eddie explained, chewing on a piece of chicken.

"Muthafucka, keep yo eyes on the damn table and out of them fuckin' chicken wings, fat muthafucka." Lavelle snatched the plate of hot wings from him.

Sieda, Lavelle's girlfriend, was laughing so hard that she almost fell out of her chair. I died laughing. She grabbed a piece of chicken and started waving it in Eddie's face. When he reached for it, she snatched it back and took a big bite in his face. We was all clownin', actin' like a bunch of fools. Sieda put another bottle of Hennessey on the table and sat on Lavelle's lap. He started dealing the cards and talking shit at the same damn time.

"Y'all know this the winnin' hand and I'm 'bout to take all y'all nigga's money. Broke ass muthafuckas." Lavelle boasted.

The game was too close to say who was gonna win. Me and Eddie were down a couple of books, but I had a couple of high cards so I thought we still had a chance of takin' the game. I was dead wrong. I threw out the ace of clubs thinkin' I was gonna take the book and Lavelle jumped up, almost making Sieda fall as he slammed a spade on the table like Ice Cube slammed the domino on the table in Boyz n the Hood, making me and Eddie bump. He started laughing all loud in our faces. As if on cue, the song "Ante Up" came on the radio and this stupid muthafucka started rapping along with the song as he collected the money off the table, telling us to ante up every time he snatched the money out of our hands. I was having so much fun that I didn't think about my problems with Venus or the damn hits on the traps, then the music cut off.

Breaking News! There was a shoot-out at Illicit Dreams Strip Club just moments ago. Witnesses say that two men opened fire on a room full of people, killing three and wounding several others. Police are on the scene now. Stay tuned for more updates as the story develops.

"WHAT THE FUCK?" Lavelle shouted. His face turned to stone as he reached for his ringing phone. Illicit Dreams was Frank's club, which meant that it was another hit on our shit.

"Yeah, what's goin' on?" he spoke into the phone. His demeanor changed from chilled to angered in a split second. "What the fuck happened?" he asked the caller. "Damn yo, Pops cool though, right?" he continued. "Aight I'll be there," he hung up.

"Yo, everything cool?" I asked. I was concerned.

"Nah, some muthafuckas shot up the club. I got to get down there. I'm telling you, muthafuckas is gunnin' for us and we might need to light a fuckin' fire under this muthafuckin' city." he fumed as he scurried around the house gathering his guns and shit.

"Baby, do what you got to do, just be careful." Sieda crooned.

"I'm always careful." he avowed. He kissed her then gave Ray and Eddie an apology for leaving in a haste. I asked if he wanted me to go with him.

"HELL NO!" he shouted, looking at me like I had lost my mind.

"I need you here to keep Sieda's ass calm." he instructed. He gave her another quick kiss, then he rushed out the door.

Sieda was sitting at the table with a blank look on her face. I walked over to her and put my arms around her.

"Everything's cool." I assured while silently praying that I wasn't lying. Sieda was visibly shaken. She'd been around Lavelle doing his business, but hearing that it was a possible war starting scared the shit outta of her. Truthfully, it scared the shit outta me too. I would lose my fuckin' mind if anything were to happen to my brother.

"Let's try not to worry, Adonis. Lavelle is a smart man. He wouldn't do anything to put himself in danger." she said. I didn't know if she was trying to reassure me or convince herself that what she was saying was true, but we both know that Lavell was loyal and would do whatever he could to protect Frank.

Lavelle

I was at a loss for words looking around as I stepped through the doors of Illicit Dreams. The smell of alcohol filled the air. All of the bottles and glasses were broken all over the room. The red walls were filled with bullet holes and the black plush moleskin lounge chairs and smoke glass top tables were either broken or turned over on the black granite floors. The mirrored ceiling over the stage was shattered. The stage lights were held up by the wires. I walked around the room shaking my head. The sound of glass cracking bounced off the walls with every step I took a step. The club was destroyed.

"What's up, Lavelle?" Tito, the bodyguard, spoke in a deep voice as we gave each other dap and a brotherly hug.

"Man, what the fuck happened?"

"Ion' know," his voice dragged as he spoke. "Two niggas was chilling on opposite sides of the club, then they just started letting loose." He shrugged his shoulders. "Frank and 'nem in the back watchin' the tapes now."

"Aight man, thanks." I dapped him up one last time and headed to the back.

"WHO THE FUCK DID THIS SHIT?" I could hear Frank's deep voice thundering through the door as I approached the office.

"HOW THE FUCK DID THIS SHIT HAPPEN?" He was shouting and pacing the floor, shaking his head. Officers Dumas and Wittman were standing by the monitors looking nervous as they followed Frank with their eyes.

"LAVELLE, LOOK AT THIS MUTHAFUCKIN' SHIT!" he shouted, pointing at the monitors. I sat down in the chair and pressed the rewind button, then I pushed play. Right before the gunmen started shooting, I noticed something.

"Wait." I pressed rewind again. I paused it when I noticed a man signaling the gunmen before they opened fire. I zoomed in to see if I could recognize the man. I told Frank to come look at the monitor. He stormed over to me. I pressed the play button and pointed out the guy that gave the signal.

"Who the fuck is that?" he asked with a confused look.

"I want every last one of them muthafuckas found. Niggas need to know I don't fuck around," he said, slamming his fist on the table. He looked at the officers on his payroll.

"Make sure my name stay the fuck outta this shit."

"Gotcha Frank, we will take care of everything." Officer Wittman assured. Frank waved his hand and dismissed them. He sat behind his desk and poured him a glass of scotch. He gulped it down and poured another one.

"How should we handle this, Pop?" Maurice asked. Me and Frank both gave him a blank stare.

"How the fuck you think I want it handled? What type of stupid ass question is that?" he questioned, staring at Maurice with a disgusted look.

"Lavelle, you see, this is why this dumb muthafucka can't be my right hand? He don't have a fuckin' brain. Dumb ass nigga." Maurice sat there with his head down and a dumb look on his face.

"Lavelle, how you gonna handle this? Pay attention, Maurice; you might learn something."

"Simple. Find the niggas and dead their asses." I stated matter-of-factly. Frank gulped down another glass of scotch.

"Dad, I got the prices from Rojas for you," Maurice beamed proudly. I gave him a confused look because he hadn't discussed that shit with me.

* * * * * * *

Maurice was always looking for a way to prove to his father that he was worthy of carrying on his legacy. I took him under my wing to teach him the ins and outs of the business. We discussed tryna do business with Rojas in the past, but Frank never trusted anyone enough to allow them to handle the exchanges until I came along and my loyalty was proven. He made me second-in-command, putting me in charge of meeting with the supplier. This was a big move for me, which was why I decided to teach Maurice what to do. It would show Frank that he was finally takin' shit serious. I didn't know why, but I had looked out for Maurice since I got in with Frank. My first and most painful kill was to protect him. I was 17.

Another boss was tryna take over Frank's territory and he wasn't havin' that. He sent his best group of guys to fuck up and take over this nigga's entire empire. Maurice wanted to go too as a way to prove himself to his father. Frank told him that he wasn't ready, that he didn't have the heart. Maurice had disappointment written all over his face and I felt some kinda way. I remembered all the times I felt disappointed behind something my father did or said. I decided that I would try to help him out. I told Frank that I would go with them to make sure Maurice could handle himself. It took some convincing, but he allowed us to go.

We crept up on the niggas all in one spot and started killin' every nigga in sight. No witnesses were Frank's orders, and we made sure of that. Maurice was runnin' behind some scared ass muthafucka and to keep my word to

Frank, I ran behind him to make sure his ass didn't get killed. A shot was fired and Maurice ducked. He pulled his gun and aimed in the direction the shot came from. I pulled mine too and walked, crouched down to the door the shot came from. Maurice came and positioned himself on the other side of the door. It was about to go down. I kicked the door in and Maurice ran in, where he was met with a bitch holding a shotgun. This stupid muthafucka balled up in the corner like a bitch. I could see that she was a second away from pulling the trigga and putting a hole through his chest. I lit this bitch up, emptying my whole clip in her ass. Maurice, who was still balled up in the corner, looked at me like I had lost my mind.

"You killed a woman, what the fuck?" he shrieked.

"Nigga, it's kill or be killed out here; if you ain't with that, then you should have stayed your bitch ass at home." I stressed, storming out of the room.

I was pissed the fuck off. I was out there risking my life so this nigga could man up. The whole time, his father was right. He had no fucking heart. At that time, killin' the bitch didn't bother me but once everything was settled, it fucked my mind up. It still bothered me til that day. I did my dirt and I took some lives with no regrets. That kill was my only regret, especially when I found out that she was *pregnant with my child. I had been fuckin' with this bitch for al'most a year and had no clue that her brother was part of Frank's rival gang, but in this business everybody's life was at stake. I knew by the look in her eyes that one of us had to die, and I'd be damned if it was gonna be me. I was picturing everything like it was happening at that moment.*

* * * * * * *

"I'm worried about who fuckin' up my shit and you talkin' 'bout some muthafuckin' deal." Frank spat, giving him a patronizing look. His loud voice bounced off the wall and damn near burst my ear drum. I snapped out of my trip down memory lane.

"If you don't get the fuck on with that shit right now." he continued.

"Frank, he got the information, just hear him out." I stated. Frank sighed with obvious frustration. He waved his hand, giving him permission to speak.

"Rojas is offering 25,000 a kilo of cocaine, 4,500 for a pound of loud, a thousand for a pound of reggie, and 125,000 a kilo of heroin." He was speaking with pride as he ran down the price of Rojas' products to his father. It was a little more than what we were paying the supplier we had now, but less than what Rojas normally charged; plus, the quality of his products were much better than the shit we were getting.

Frank sat back in his chair rubbing his chin with his brows frowned. He looked like he was in deep thought.

"Lavelle, I need you to handle this. It's a big deal, you need to meet with Rojas." he reiterated.

"Frank, Maurice stepped up a lot; I think he can handle this." I replied.

"Yeah Pop, I'm the one who got the deal." Maurice pointed out.

"Ok, he can handle it but you need to be there. If this goes wrong, Lavelle, it's on your head." I knew he meant what he said. Frank was ruthless and had no problem killing anybody, including his own flesh and blood. One time, Frank's cousin Jimmy came up short on Frank's dope and thought it was cool 'cause they were blood relatives. Frank found out and blew his fuckin' brains out at the park in broad daylight in front of hundreds of witnesses, and then paid for Jimmy's funeral. Frank poured himself another drink and we discussed a little more business, then he dismissed us.

I left the office feeling the pressure. I was putting my ass on the line once again for Maurice, and I wasn't sure he deserved it. No matter how hard he tried to impress his father, he always ended up fuckin' shit up.

"Lavelle, thanks for trustin' me man, for real and no matter what my father believes, I don't need you to hold my hand with this deal. Rojas knows and trusts me. I think I should be the one dealing with him." Maurice said as we walked to my car.

"Look Maurice, you should have told me about the deal before takin' it to your father. I needed to know the details so that I could make the decision regarding whether or not we'd go to Frank with that offer. It sounds good, but I need to make sure we are getting the best deal." I stated.

"My bad man, but it was a take it or leave it deal. Rojas wasn't up for any more negotiations," he shrugged his shoulders. "Am I still handling the deal?" he asked.

"Maurice, you gotta come through with this deal and be on point with this shit. My muthafuckin' head on the line, and I'll be damned if you fuck shit up for me. I need to be at the first few meetings but you can still handle the deal. If it gets to be too much or you need me to handle shit, you better let me know." I gave him dap and headed to home.

When I walked in the door, Adonis was laid back on my sofa watching the news. The story about the shooting at the club was on. Adonis shook his head, looking at the pictures of the damage on the screen.

"Man, this shit is crazy." he said as I walked toward him.

"I know that shit got Frank on edge." I glanced at the images on the screen, then told Adonis that I was going to let Sieda know that I was home and come talk to him.

After making sure that Sieda knew that I was cool and choppin' it up with her a bit, I went back out in the living room to have my conversation with Adonis. I didn't know or even care to know everything that was going on in his relationship. All I knew was he was fuckin' up a good thing. Venus was a good girl and no matter what the situation was, she didn't deserve to be treated the way that Adonis had been treating her. I got us each a glass of 1738 and sat beside him on the sofa.

"What's going on with you, man?" I asked as I passed him his glass.

"I don't know; I just been feeling a little stressed." he replied.

"About?" I questioned. He let out a sigh then leaned back on the sofa.

"A lot of shit. It's hard for me to do what I have to do in business and do everything Venus wants me to do." He rubbed his hand over his head. "It's like I can't get shit right." he added.

"First, let me remind you that home life is always first. When Venus needs you, be there. Business is secondary." I reiterated.

"Business is how I make the money that's needed to take care of home." he stated.

"Is she complaining about money? No, all she doing is asking you for a little help when needed. It's your responsibility to make sure her needs and wants are taken care of, just like she takes care of yours." I lectured. He nodded in agreement.

"If you need me to step in and help with business, let me know. This my shit too, we in this together" I reminded him. "At the end of the day, we all we got so don't ever hesitate to call if you need me." He nodded. I gave him a brotherly hug then sent his ass home.

Adonis

I really didn't want to leave Lavelle's house. I needed a break from the tension in my house. I was tired of all the arguing. It had gotten to the point where we were purposely hitting each other below the belt. There had been times when I wanted to jack her lil' ass up to put some fear in her, but I knew if I did that she would try her best to beat my ass, then I would end up putting my hands on her. That was something I would never do because only fuck boys hit women. Shit, I had to be honest; Venus' crazy ass would probably kill my ass in my sleep. I swear that girl showed no fear, not even when that nigga tried to fuck her when we were younger. Venus stabbed his ass, then the next day Lavelle and I rode around until we found his nasty ass. Venus begged me not to kill him, so we beat the nigga within an inch of his life and put that nigga in a coma. They found his ass barely breathing in an alley the next morning. I would do anything for Venus, which was why this shit between me and her was driving me crazy, and with everything else on my mind I was mentally exhausted.

I pulled up at the Embassy Suites Hotel in Northwest hoping that they had a room, and they did. I opened the door to my king suite, tossed my keys on the table, pulled the curtains back on the big ass window, and stood there looking at the view of the Washington Monument. The lights from the surrounding buildings were glowing, making the lights from the monument look even brighter. The dome of the Capitol stood out in a far distance as the moon and stars lit up around the entire scene. It was a beautiful view, making me love my fucked up city even more. I admired the view for a little while longer, then sat on the sofa and turned on the TV. I started watching the news and my eyes began to feel heavy. I blinked rapidly, tryna stay awake but I was tired as shit. I turned the TV off and went into the room. I took off my clothes, leaving on my boxers and beater, then stretched out on the king size bed. As soon as my head hit the pillow, I fell asleep.

I woke up the next morning feeling refreshed. I reached over and grabbed my phone from the table. I had ten missed calls from Venus, five from Lavelle, a few from Loco, and notifications that I had voicemails. I stretched then went into the bathroom. After emptying my bladder, I washed my face and brushed my teeth. I went back into the room, picked up my phone, and checked my voicemails. Lavelle left one telling me to call him, then Venus left one asking me to please call her because she was worried. Knowing that all the voicemails were from them two, I exited out of voicemail. I got dressed and headed downstairs to get some breakfast. As soon as I sat down, my phone started ringing.

"Yeah." I answered.

"Yeah, nigga? YEAH, that's all you can say? My muthafuckin' ass been calling you all fuckin' night worried. Where the fuck you at?" Lavelle asked, yelling into the phone.

"Chillin' nigga." I replied nonchalantly.

"Chillin'? Wit who? You betta not be with no bitch."

"Lavelle, chill wit that shit, you know I don't fuck around on my girl. I just needed some space so I stayed at a hotel."

"SPACE? You sound like a fuckin' fool. Why the fuck you need space muthafucka, you the one fuckin' up, talkin' 'bout you need space. That girl ain't do shit but love yo dirty ass drawls and try to make you do right by her. Man, take yo ass home and deal with the shit YOU created. Got that girl calling me in the middle of the fuckin' night worried 'bout yo simple ass." he ranted. He continued going on and on ripping into my ass. I half-way listened as I continued to eat my bacon, eggs, sausage, waffles, grits, and homemade fries. After breakfast, I checked out and headed home.

I walked in the door and Venus jumped in my arms. Tear stains were on her moist cheeks. Her eyes were bloodshot and puffy. Her hair was all over her head and it was obvious that she'd been crying all night. All of sudden, she pulled away from me and slapped the shit outta me.

"Don't you ever do that shit to me again, I was worried sick." she sniffed.

"I needed time to think." I responded.

"So you couldn't call or even answer when I called? Since when do you not come home? Is that where we at now? And what the fuck you need to think about?" She was firing off question after question, not giving me any time to respond.

"To be honest, I had to think about us."

"What about us?" she asked with a scrunched up face, looking confused.

"I was thinking that maybe we needed a break from each other, and—"

"A break?" she cut me off. "Let's get one thing straight right now. There are no breaks for us. Either we together or we not, simple as that. We been together too damn long to need a fuckin' break. Fuck you talkin' 'bout?"

"Baby, if you shut yo mouth for one second I can finish." I chuckled. She shifted on one leg and folded her arms, giving me her full attention.

"I realized that I'm at fault for all this. I let too much shit fuck with my head and fuck up my priorities. I don't need a break; I just need to step up." I confessed. I wrapped my arms around her waist. "I love you, and I'm sorry for making you worry."

"Aren't you tired of apologizing for doing dumb shit?" she asked.

"Shut up and kiss me." I replied as I pulled her closely and kissed her.

"Harmony still sleep?" I asked. She nodded yes. I backed her against the wall, pulled off my t-shirt that she had on, then slid down my pants. I lifted her up on the wall and thrust deep inside of her.

"I could never leave this pussy, it's too damn good." She playfully slapped me.

"Shut up and fuck me." she moaned. I sucked her lip into my mouth then kissed her as I thrust deeper inside of her.

Instead of running the streets, I decided to take my family out for the day. It had been a while since I did that. I enjoyed my night alone at the hotel but I ain't gon lie, rolling over and searching for Venus in the middle of the night and she wasn't there was a reality check for my ass. I couldn't imagine my life without her.

Venus

I couldn't remember the last time Adonis spent the day with me and Harmony but he wanted to go out on a family outing today. He told me about the view of the monument from the window of the hotel and decided that we should go to The National Mall, a national park kinda like a boulevard that was home to some of the best free museums and memorials in the country, like The Washington Monument, Smithsonian Institute, The Lincoln Memorial, The Martin Luther King Jr. Memorial, The National Museum of Natural History, and the National Museum of African American History and Culture. The National Mall was where Dr. Martin Luther King Jr. gave his famous *I Have a Dream* speech. It was a great place to visit to learn a lot about our country's history.

After visiting The Martin Luther King Jr. Memorial and taking pictures, we went to The National Museum of African American History and Culture and took a tour. It was like going back in time. I was amazed looking at all the historical objects as well as learning a lot about the culture, the stories, and the histories of our people, and how African Americans had impacted freedom struggles around the world. It was truly amazing. After that, we decided to stop at

Potbelly's sandwich shop. Potbelly's gave that old-time feeling being that it was an antique shop turned into a sandwich shop. Its atmosphere was fun, friendly and great for families. Adonis ordered a sandwich called *A Wreck*. It had salami, roast beef, turkey, ham, and Swiss cheese on it and he ordered the big size.

"Really, Adonis? All those meats on one sandwich?" I asked. He laughed, then gave me a flirtatious look.

"You should know by now I'm a carnivore." he snickered, then flicked his tongue in and out of his mouth like he was licking my pearl.

"You so nasty." I giggled, thinking about what that tongue did to me.

"Wait until we get home, I'll remind you of my flesh-eating skills." That sent a rush of tingles in my pearl and all of a sudden, I couldn't wait to get home.

Harmony was knocked out when we got home. Adonis put her in her bed, then came in the room. I was sitting on the bed taking my shoes off. He walked into the room and closed the door. He pushed me back on the bed, took my jeans off, put my feet on the bed, and started feastin' on my pussy. Not only did he do what he said, he was reminding me that he was truly a carnivore, but he also reminded me that he was an animal in bed. I ain't gon' lie, he fucked the shit outta me. He made me have so many orgasms that I could hardly stand and my legs were too wobbly to even go to the bathroom. I came out of the bathroom and got back in bed thinking that we were finished, but I thought wrong. Adonis turned me on my side and lifted my leg on his shoulder, then entered me.

"Adonis, I can't take no more." I protested, trying to put my leg down.

"I ain't tryna hear that shit, this my pussy." he said in a low tone as he thrust deeper inside of me while rubbing my clit.

"Fuck Adonis, I'm already about to cum." I moaned. His strokes were now hard and fast and after about ten minutes, my body was shaking out of control. He continued his stroke until he released inside of me.

"I'll let you rest for now, but we nowhere near finished." he told me, then smacked me on the ass. He turned on the TV. I wrapped my leg around his, laid my head on his chest, and dozed off. I was asleep for maybe an hour before I was woken up by Adonis thrusting inside of me. His stamina today was off the chain; I could hardly keep up with him. As soon as we finished another round, I went to sleep.

"Bitch, get yo ass up. We supposed to be going to Tyson's Galleria today; remember, a little retail therapy?"

Kay Kay said loudly into the phone. I blinked my eyes a few times trying to focus. I looked over at the clock and it read 9:10 am.

"Bitch, I know you fuckin' hear me, wake the fuck up!" she shouted.

"Oook, Oook Kaylee, I'm up." I whined.

"Yeah, well you betta be. It's a long drive and bitch I'm on the way."

She hung up. I turned over and noticed Adonis wasn't in the bed. I yawned, then stuck one foot over the side of the bed. I stretched, then dragged myself out of bed.

Adonis came out of the bathroom still a little wet, wearing nothing but a towel. He looked sexy as hell. Normally, I would have jumped on his ass real quick, but my box was sore from the all-night pounding he put on it last night. He noticed me watching him and took his towel off. He grabbed his dick and asked if I wanted some. I shook my head no.

"You lookin' at me like you want some of this dick." He snickered, walking over toward me. I hopped off of the bed fast as shit.

"I can't, I have to go. Kay Kay is on the way." I said, rushing to the bathroom. He grabbed me and snatched me into his arms, grabbing my ass.

"You know I don't give a fuck if she on the way." He pulled me closer and kissed me. He walked me to the bed, still kissing me and gripping my ass. I tripped and fell back on the bed. He grabbed my ankles and lifted my legs on his shoulders. He was just about to enter me.

"Mommy." Harmony called knocking on the door. He hopped up quick and slid his basketball shorts on. I was happy as hell. I ran to the door, snatching it open.

"Mommy, I'm hungry." she whined, rubbing her little eyes.

"Ok, Mommy is going to get us dressed, then we can grab some breakfast on the way to Grandma's house, ok?"

"Oook." she whined and trotted back to her room.

"You lucky. I was about to tear that ass up." Adonis teased, smacking me on my ass. He went in the closet to pick out something to wear and I headed to the bathroom to take a quick shower.

Kay Kay was sitting on my bed when I got out of the shower. Adonis grabbed his phone and gave me a quick kiss, then left.

"Bye Adonis." Kay Kay said, waving her hand. "Girl, hurry up," she demanded, rushing me. She decided to help Harmony get dressed while waiting for me to get ready so we could hurry up. I quickly got dressed, fluffed my curls with my fingers, then we left.

As much as I loved shopping, I was ready to leave two hours after we got there. I was feeling sluggish. Kay Kay's happy ass was energetic as hell, bouncing around the mall like she'd drunk a six-pack of Red Bull. Since I hadn't eaten anything, we decided to go to The Cheesecake Factory to eat. It was packed as usual and I really didn't feel like waiting for a table. I was so glad that we were able to get a table quick, 'cause I was still kinda tired from last night. Sitting at the table, she started talking about Loco. She was going on and on about how crazy and funny he was. Her eyes twinkled, her face lit up, and her smile grew wider just mentioning his name.

"Girl, you feeling Loco like that?" I asked, amused. I had never seen her so giddy about a man before.

"Like what?" she answered in a high-pitched voice.

"Don't play dumb, you know you want Loco." I pointed out. She covered her face like a little girl and nodded yes.

"But when we were talkin' the other day about relationships, he told me that he didn't want one. He said that he believed in karma, and he felt like if he got into a serious relationship something gon' happen to pay him back for all the shit he done." she told me.

"Do you think you can deal with that?" I asked.

"I don't know." she shrugged her shoulders. "That's why I'm kinda keeping my distance but damn it's hard as hell. He is so fuckin' fine and sexy. I don't know if I can stay away," she added. I was speechless.

After eating, I was more energetic and ready to shop. Kay Kay saw these jeans in the window of the BCBG; we went inside the store so she could try them on. I found a couple of things that I liked myself. I picked up a shirt and held it against my body to see how it looked. I felt someone wrap their arms around me from behind and kissed my neck. I turned around and came face to face with Adonis.

"Hey baby, what are you doing here?" I asked, surprised.

"Me and Loco just came from Hugo Boss and I saw you, so I came to get a kiss." he answered as I wrapped my arms around his neck.

"What's up Venus, Kay Kay." Loco spoke as he approached us. Kay Kay blushed before speaking, then rushed to the dressing room. As I was showing Adonis the clothes that I was buying, Loco disappeared.

Kay Kay

I couldn't take the intense way that Loco was staring at me when he spoke to me and Venus. After speaking, I turned on my heels and made my way to the dressing room to try on the outfit I wanted to buy. I pulled off my shirt, then my jeans and was standing in the mirror wearing nothing but a bra and panties. I reached for the jeans that I wanted to try on. Loco slipped through the curtain, startling me. I quickly tried to cover myself with the jeans that I had in my hands.

"Don't cover up, you look sexy as hell." he complimented, snatching the jeans from my hands. He gave me a half-smile, then stepped closer to me. The way he was licking his lips and scanning my body with his eyes made my body temperature rise, and I started to feel nervous. I had never wanted anybody like I wanted him.

"Loco, you have to get out; you can't be in here." I told him, giving him a pleading look.

"What you tell me on the phone the other night? I'll go crazy if you even let me touch it for five minutes." he repeated.

Ever since the day we met, we'd been talking on the phone a couple times a week and whenever we ran into each other, we flirted a little. He, of course, would come at me on some *I wanna fuck* type shit. I would talk shit to him, telling him how niggas I fucked in the past got whipped, or how he probably couldn't handle me if I gave it to him just to make him more eager to get it. Being in this dressing room right here right now, half-naked with little space in between us had a bitch feeling horny as hell.

"Loco, what are you doing? Stop." I protested as he backed me into the corner away from the mirror. He slid his hands up and down my side. Moving my panties to the side, he slid his finger inside me and started circling my pearl with his thumb. His thumb glided smoothly as my juices started dripping down his fingers.

"Please stop." I begged in a low tone. He stuck two more fingers inside of me. His hands were so big that it felt like he stuck a dick in me. I gasped. He slowly licked my lips, then kissed me. As our tongues danced around in each other's mouth, he shoved his fingers deeper inside of my wetness.

"AAAAHHHH," I moaned as I wrapped my arms around his neck, lifting my leg so he could go deeper.

While fondling my g-spot, he put a little more pressure on my pearl. I felt trembles growing deep in my stomach. I squeezed his neck a little tighter. I laid my head against the wall as I ground on his fingers.

"Yeah, baby; this gon' be my pussy. You gon' give it to me?" he asked. I nodded my head yes.

"Tell me you want me." he commanded in a sexy low tone.

"I want you." I whispered as I moaned, feeling light-headed.

"If you want me, come to my house later." he said, making my body tense. My knees were weak and trembling and I knew I was about to cum. All of a sudden, Loco stopped.

"What are you doing?" I asked, breathing heavy as my body continued trembling.

"Winning the challenge." he smirked, sucking my juices off his fingers. He gave me a quick kiss and hurried out of the dressing room.

"What the fuck just happened?" I asked myself, trying to wrap my head around what just happened.

It took me a few minutes to get myself together, and trying on the outfit was no longer on my mind. I stepped into the hallway of the dressing area, looking around and hoping no one heard what we were doing in the dressing room. I saw Venus, Adonis, and Loco standing at the rack of shirts that were right in front of the dressing room. I made eye contact with Loco and he smirked, biting on his bottom lip. I blushed. I swear if I was white, my cheeks would have been red as hell. I quickly looked away and my eyes fell right on Venus. She was giving me a look that let me know she knew what happened. How could she not? I couldn't hide the guilt that showed all over my face.

"So, did the outfit fit you?" she asked in a sarcastic tone.

"Umm, I decided not to get it." I lied as I made a quick dash out of the store, making sure not to look Loco in the face.

My phone vibrated and it was a text from Loco giving me his address and a time to be at his house. I exited the text and put my phone in my purse. I looked up and Loco was standing right in front of me. Venus and Adonis were a short distance behind him.

"Don't be late." he ordered as Adonis got closer. He told Venus he would see her later and gave her a quick peck on the cheek before walking away.

"What the fuck happened in that dressing room? You came out looking all flustered and shit," Venus questioned with her hands on her hips.

"Girl, I have no idea." I said, shaking my head. Venus gave me a look of disbelief but decided to drop the subject.

As we walked out of the mall, I started thinking about Loco and his magical fingers. I still felt them inside of me.

"Why in the hell you keep checkin' the damn time?" Venus asked as she pulled her knees to her chest. We were chilling at her house talking about the frustrations she was feeling in her relationship. I wasn't paying her too much attention, not because I wasn't interested, but because my mind was on something else—going to see Loco.

"Vee, I have to leave. I got something to do, but I'll come over tomorrow to finish talking," I informed her as I grabbed my purse and my keys, and headed home to take a bath before going to Loco's house.

As soon as I walked in the door, Loco was all over me. He pinned me against the wall by my wrist with my hands above my head and kissed me. He was using his tongue to literally fuck my mouth. Flicking his tongue in and out my mouth slowly, his lips barely touched mine and I could feel brushes of his breath sweeping across my lips. I was drowning in pleasure. He slowly traced my lips with his tongue and my box instantly started throbbing with excitement as his lust-filled gazed sent shivers through my body. Still holding my wrist with one hand, he slid his other hand down the side of my body. He sucked my bottom lip into his mouth as he slid his hand down my pants.

"Damn, you wet already." he whispered, stroking my freshly shaven pleasure box.

I could feel my body heat rise and my lips swell from arousal as he stuck his fingers deeper inside of me. He took his fingers out and stuck them in his mouth, slowly sucking my juices off of them. He looked sexy as hell and I was turned on.

"MMMMM, I'm about to feast on this pussy." he said in a sexy low tone. He grabbed my hand and led me to his bedroom. He pulled a chair to the middle of the room and sat down.

"Take off yo clothes," he demanded.

I started taking off my clothes and he stopped me.

"Do it slow, I want you to strip for me." he instructed in a deep husky tone.

He sat back in the chair slouched to one side with his arm hanging over the back, and his hand on his chin in the thinker pose. I started slowly taking off my clothes and moving my hips in a sexy slow circle. His small eyes narrowed as he watched my every move. Once I was nude, he motioned for me to come to him. I took my time walking in my sexiest strut. He was looking at me as if he was admiring a thing of beauty. He pulled me down by the back of my neck and kissed me passionately, then turned me around and sat me on his lap backward. Sucking and lightly biting on my neck, he slid his hands up my body from my ankles until he was cupping my breasts, twirling my nipples between his fingers and thumbs. I moaned softly as quivers shot through my body. He opened his legs, opening my legs wider with his legs, then inserted his fingers in my box as he circled my pearl with his thumb. My body had so many sensations going through it at once that my head was spinning. I was more stimulated and sexually aroused than I had ever been in my life.

"I'm about to cum." I moaned, laying my head back on his shoulder. My body started trembling.

"I know." He breathed as he sucked the side of my neck.

He picked me up off his lap and turned me toward him. He lifted one of my legs on his shoulder and planted his strong tongue in my pleasure box, circling my pearl with his tongue. I threw my head back and closed my eyes as I grabbed a hand full of his dreads. He wrapped his arm around my other leg and lifted me off the ground. I let out a loud moan as he continued devouring my pussy. I felt trembles deep in my stomach, my toes were curled, and I felt light-headed. I grabbed his head, pushing him deeper as the trembles in my stomach became more intense.

"AAHHHHH!" I moaned loudly. As I climaxed, he slurped up every bit of my juices.

"Grab your ankles." He spoke with authority, turning me on even more.

He turned me around and nudged me. I bent forward and grabbed my ankles. He spread my ass cheeks and started eating my ass. It was an unusual but unbelievable feeling. It felt better than eating my box. My knees wobbled, almost making me fall forward. I had to place my hands on the floor for support. He was slapping my cheeks with both hands, squeezing them while flicking his tongue in and out of my hole, sending shockwaves of ecstasy through my body as I came again. He grabbed me by the waist and walked me over to the bed. I was feeling intoxicated. Like Beyoncé, I was drunk in love. He took off his clothes and my eyes grew bigger looking at the size of his dick.

Loco

The surprised look on Kay Kay's face let me know that she wasn't ready for the monster that I'd just unleashed from my pants. Her big brown, bliss-filled doe eyes were open as wide as they could get. She looked like she'd seen a ghost and was scared outta her mind. The truth was, she should've been. I laughed a little on the inside as I watched her chest rise and fall rapidly from her labored breathing. My eyes scanned her body; the darkness of her areola against her mocha skin tone made her hard nipples stand out even more. She licked her juicy Meagan Good-looking lips like she was telling me to come fuck the shit outta her, and I was more than happy to oblige.

I climbed on top of her and kissed those juicy soft lips of hers as I opened her legs. I thrust deep inside of her. She gasped. I didn't move; I wanted her to adjust to my size before I put a beat down on her pussy. I felt her muscles relax around my dick as the tension in her body disappeared. I pushed her legs behind her head, got in the push-up position, and plunged deep inside her.

"OH SSSHHIT!" she cried out, exhaling the breath that she was holding in. I sped up my pace, thrusting harder and deeper into her box. She grabbed my arms and squeezed so tight that her nails left dents in my skin.

"AAAH AAAAH AAAH!" she howled with each stroke.

She put her hands on the bed and tried to scoot up and away. She was trying to run from the dick and I wasn't about to let that happen. I scooted up with her. She did it again and so did I. We continued scooting up until her back was against the headboard.

"You can't get away from me, baby." I said. I put her legs on my shoulders and pinned her arms down, then sat up on my knees and plunged into her roughly.

"OH GOD!" she yelled.

"Nah baby, don't call him to help you outta this." I sneered. I sped up my pace and she started bouncing off the headboard. Her loud moans of pleasure were mixed with the loud smacking sounds of her pussy, filling the room. I kissed her to quiet her some.

"FUUUUCK!" she screamed as she had another orgasm.

"Turn that ass over," I ordered, slapping her on her thigh. She moved lazily as she turned and got on all fours.

"OH OH SHIT OH FUCK!" she babbled, not knowing what to say as I held her by her waist and stroked her hard and fast. She reached her hands back and tried to push me away.

"Why you running?" I asked.

"It-it HHHURTS!" she groaned.

"It hurts? Ain't this what you wanted?" I questioned.

"YYYEEEESSS!" she whimpered.

"Then you better learn how to handle this dick. Ain't no muthafuckin' runnin', not after all that shit you was talking," I husked. "In fact, throw that ass back." I demanded.

I pulled her hair and gripped her around her throat and said, "This my shit." as I pounded her harder. She gripped the sheets tightly as I continued my stroke.

Her mouth was stuck open in an O shape; her breathing was heavy as I sped up my pace. She closed her eyes and her body started jerking. I wrapped my arm around her waist and pulled her up into a sitting position while still gripping her throat. He limp body fell against my body and her head dropped on my shoulder. I changed my stroke into a slow grind. She let out a zombie-like moan and the next thing I knew, she was squirting and her juices were running down my lap. I gripped her tightly as I changed my slow grind into quick, hard strokes until I exploded. I let her go and her limp body fell flat on the bed into a pool of her own juices. I chuckled to myself, then told her to get up so I could change the sheets. She didn't move. I tried shaking her but she still didn't move. I picked her up and placed her on a blanket on the floor, then changed the sheets. I picked her up again, put her back in the bed, and put the blanket over her. She stayed in the same position the whole time. She was in a coma-like sleep. If I hadn't heard her snoring lightly, I would have thought shawty was dead.

I took a quick shower, then climbed in bed. I wasn't used to having bitches sleep in my bed. My motto was *find 'em, fuck 'em, and flee,* but there was something about the peaceful way Kay Kay looked sleeping that made me let her stay. I kissed shawty on her cheek, turned off the light, and closed my eyes.

Lavelle

Two more traps had been hit and we still hadn't figured out who was behind this shit. Loco, Smoke, and the other hittas on our team had been runnin' up on muthafuckas and everything else they could think of, tryna get information. Nobody knew who these niggas was. I was about to start bodying niggas until I got some answers. They were fuckin' with my money and that shit didn't fly with me. I sat at my desk tryna put some pieces together in my own mind. I really thought Loco and Adonis were right. All this shit was coming from home, which meant I had some snakes in my yard. I was about to cut my grass.

I called a meeting to start promptly at 11 am. I hated for my time to be wasted so I wanted everyone there by 10: 45 am. Just like Frank, I looked at tardiness as a form of disrespect and a sign of disloyalty. He taught me to run a tight camp. *Loyalty or death* was the code Frank lived by. Once the streets realized that he was quick with his shit and I, his right-hand man, had an *I don't give a fuck attitude*, muthafuckas came correct or didn't come at all.

"Click, click."

The sound of my gun cocking got niggas' attention quick and fast. The chatter amongst the men ceased. I sat at the head of the table with cold, dark eyes peering into the crowd of men. I was seeing which one of them couldn't look me in the eye, then I thought about something my mother used to say. A dog would look down when they'd done wrong, but a snake would look you dead in the eyes. Adonis came over and took his seat right next to mine as the meeting began.

"So, you niggas think I'm a fuckin' joke?" I asked, slamming my fist down on the table, making all of the men jump a bit.

"I'm confused. Are we not all eating?" I questioned, searching the silent room with rage-filled eyes. My nose was flaring as I bit down on my bottom lip. "Some of you muthafuckas think you have balls the size of watermelons, but I'm the nigga that will cut those muthafuckas off. Niggas on the streets lookin' at us like we soft 'cause niggas fuckin' our shit up and we can't get answers. I had a deal in place with Rojas and he backed down because we can't seem to handle business. The fuck that look like?" I stood up and started pacing the floor.

"How the fuck we gonna run shit if we can't get our own shit in order? We out here losing money...nah, we ain't losing shit—y'all letting bitch ass niggas take our shit. Muthafuckas gunnin' for us and here we are shakin' blocks down, offin' niggas, and still no fucking answers. What the fuck do that say about us as a fuckin' TEAM?" I threw the glass against the wall, shattering it into pieces. I waved my hands in the air out of frustration as I sat down.

"I have my team out here doin' everything they can to find out who coming for us and like Lavelle said, the streets ain't sayin' shit. That lead me to believe that we have a snake in our grass, and we have zero tolerance for that shit. If you don't know the value of loyalty, then you can't appreciate the cost of betrayal. I never understood that quote until now. We've been betrayed and it's costing us a lot." Adonis spoke with authority, explaining the circumstances to the men.

"And I'm about to clean house." I added, cutting in. "I dealt with disloyal muthafuckas before, and y'all niggas can go to Rock Creek Cemetery and ask them how. I have no problem with takin' a nigga's entire bloodline. I'll get to the bottom of this shit and when I do, somebody gots to pay." I spoke with clarity as I informed the crew of my intentions.

"One last thing I want y'all mutherfuckas to remember is that the only people I owe my loyalty to is the ones that never made me question theirs, and I'm questioning all y'all niggas loyalty."

I dismissed everyone. I knew I wasn't gon' find out shit during this meeting; it wasn't about that. I wanted them niggas to know that I knew one of them was behind this shit, and I wanted to let whoever it was know that their life was about to be over. I had Maurice stay behind just to inform him of my intentions with Rojas.

"Maurice, after I clean house and get shit in order, I want you back on this deal with Rojas and I want you to set up the meeting, but I'm gonna be the one that handle business. Got me?"

"Yea, I got you." Maurice answered in a flat voice. I dismissed him. I was tense and I needed to relax. I had to regroup so that I could be level-headed enough to put an end to all the bullshit going on.

"Lavelle man, I'm not feeling Maurice, for real. Did you notice how he just responded? He seemed a little off," Adonis said, sitting on the corner of my desk. "Look. I'm not around that nigga that much, but I swear he rubs me the wrong way," he added.

"Adonis, Maurice is under a lot of pressure. I'm making him work hard to gain Frank's respect and he's been putting in work, but Frank still don't show him respect."

"Maybe because he knows his son," he pointed out. "Look bruh, I know you took on the father figure role model with me but you can't do that with him. You ain't his daddy. You been helping this nigga out since y'all was teens and he still ain't catching on. Look at me, I was 16 when I started in this game and look how much I accomplished." he lectured.

"So now you lecturing me huh, lil' bro?" I chuckled. I got up and put him in a headlock like I used to do when he would say some slick shit out of his mouth when we were kids.

"Damn nigga, I almost can't do this shit no more, you all grown and shit." I laughed.

"Yeah, remember you taught me everything I know." He replied.

"Lil' nigga, I'll still beat yo ass." I playfully punched him in the chest.

"You can try." he snickered. "But on some real shit Lavelle, watch Maurice because if anything happens to you out here fuckin' with him, I'm killing everything moving," he stated in a serious tone.

"You don't have to worry about that, ain't nothing gon' happen to me." I assured. I gave him a brotherly hug, then he left.

After Adonis left, I sat back in my seat stroking the hairs on my chin as I thought about what Adonis had said to me about watching Maurice. I loved my lil' brother and I knew he meant well, but I didn't really understand why he was adamant about me keeping an eye on Maurice. I sighed and took a shot of Tequila, just thinking. Maybe Adonis was right and I should keep an eye on Maurice. That nigga really could be a wolf in sheep's clothing, but I really didn't see how that shit could even be possible. That nigga was still practically scared of his own damn shadow. Fuck it, I had more important shit to think about than to be looking after Maurice's timid ass. I had to focus on finding out who'd been hitting us up and dead their ass.

Adonis

I couldn't shake the uneasy feeling I was having after leaving the meeting with Lavelle. Something about the entire situation wasn't sitting right with me. As smart as my brother was, sometimes I felt like he was blinded by his own loyalty. Maybe he was more loyal to Frank and Maurice than they were to him. I hoped he listened to what I was saying about Maurice and watched him with a close eye. I knew I would. I didn't want to jump out there and accuse the muthafucka of anything, but for some reason—and I couldn't put my finger on it—he seemed shady at times. Maybe it was just me and the fact that I didn't trust no muthafuckin' body in this business. I grabbed my phone off the passenger seat and dialed Beans' number. Beans was the nigga I went to when I needed information. He was an ex-marine as well as a private detective, which meant that he could get information on anybody. I impatiently waited as the phone rang several times in my ear. I hated when niggas took forever to answer the got damn phone.

"Beans." he answered out of breath.

"What the fuck took you so damn long to answer the fuckin' phone?" I asked with an attitude.

"I was in the John, nigga," he replied.

Beans was an old, fat *Otis from the TV show Martin* looking muthafucker, and I didn't need the visual of him doing anything in the bathroom.

"Nigga you could've kept that shit to yo self, I don't need to hear shit about you in the fuckin' john, and who the fuck says john anyway? You old mothafucka," I laughed.

"Would you rather I said I was takin' a shit?" he asked with a slight chuckle.

"Fuck outta here with that nasty shit nigga." I blurted.

"Why you on my line anyway, Youngblood?" he asked in a serious tone, putting an end to our usual back and forth before we got down to business.

"I need you to get info on Maurice Lewis."

"Frank's son?"

"Yeah and Beans, this between you and me. Don't say shit to my brother."

"Gotcha." We hung up.

Turning onto the Suitland Parkway exit, I decided to go see my mother. Pulling up to her house, I noticed a strange car parked in her driveway. I jumped out of my car, making sure I had my hammer on my waist as I dashed to her door. I rang the doorbell five times in a row.

"Who ringing my doorbell like they lost their damn mind?" my mother yelled from the other side the door.

"It's me, Ma," I chuckled. I heard shuffling in the house. I banged on the door.

"Yo, open this door" I shouted. She swung open the door.

"First of all, don't pop your ass over here banging on my door, what's wrong with you?" she asked with a frowned up face.

"Who in your house?" I asked, ignoring her attitude.

"None of your damn business, that's who in my house; what you doing here?"

"Can I come in and not stand at your door like I'm a Jehovah's Witness or something?"

"No Adonis, you can't come in. I have company and you should have called. With that being said, I will call you later." She stood there with her arms folded and a mug on her face.

"Why you being all secretive and stuff? You got a nigga in there or something?" I questioned, faking like I was joking but I was dead ass. She betta not have had no nigga up in her house and I didn't know who the hell he was.

"I don't mess with niggas, I mess with men; but if you must know, I am entertaining a friend and I am being rude, so I'm going to tell you one last time. I will call you later, goodbye." She closed the door in my face.

I couldn't believe she'd slammed the door in my face like I was trying to sell her a magazine subscription or something. I promise, if she wasn't my mother and would've beat the shit outta my ass, I would have kicked her damn door in. I took a picture of the car and the tag number of the car in her driveway, then I hopped in my car and called Lavelle. When he answered, I started rambling off the details of what just happened.

"Man, you got bigger shit to worry about than who momma fuckin." he stated. He spoke like he wasn't concerned at all.

"Nigga, I don't want no muthafucka slidin' up in my mother, fuck wrong with you?" My ass was pissed.

"What? Stop actin' like a lil' ass boy. She's a grown ass woman, fuck you think she doing? Ain't that how we got here, stupid ass?"

"Fuck you Lavelle, I don't want to hear that shit."

"Boy, get off my line with this shit, go the fuck home. Yo ass shouldn't have popped up on her, that's why she slammed the door in yo fuckin' face."

"Bye." I hung up. I was speeding on the highway heading home, mad as hell. I couldn't think about no nigga tryna stick his shriveled up lil' dick in my mother.

Venus was sitting on the sofa cracking up laughing when I told her about my mother. I didn't know why everybody found this shit funny.

"Awww baby, don't be mad. Momma got to get her Stella on." Venus giggled.

"Fuck you mean?" I asked confused about what she meant.

"She got to get her groove back," she chuckled as she moved her hips like she was having sex. That turned me on.

"You wanna get your groove back?" I asked, pulling her closer to me.

"Always." she stated as I climbed on top of her and kissed her passionately.

"Hi Daddy." Harmony said, running into the living room and jumping on me.

I gave Venus a quick peck and told her that we would finish later. I turned around and put Harmony on my lap, attacking her with kisses. She started giggling with her little cute snorting giggle like her mother's, trying to play fight me.

"Oh, you going like that?" I flipped her onto the sofa and started tickling her.

"I love you, Daddy." she giggled. I swear a tear formed in my eye. I loved this little girl more than life itself.

"I love you too, my little cookie monster." I embraced her tightly, then laid her back on the sofa.

"Gimme cookies." I said in a deep monster-like voice, trying to mimic Cookie Monster from Sesame Street before I attacked her with kisses.

"Y'all are so silly." Venus giggled as she answered her ringing phone.

"Yeah, I was about to get ready now," I heard her saying to Kay Kay. She got off the phone and rushed upstairs. I sent Harmony to her play room, then went upstairs.

I walked into the room and saw that she was in the closet picking out something to wear. She came out of the closet with a pair of black ripped moto jeans and a black, off-shoulder top draped over her arm. In her hand, she carried her Very Riche pumps by Christian Louboutin. She laid her outfit out on the bed, then went to the dresser to get a pair of panties. She moved around the room like she didn't see me standing there.

"Ummm, where the hell you going?" I asked, leaning against the dresser with my legs crossed at the ankles and my hand on the dresser.

"I'm going for drinks with Kay Kay," she replied, grabbing her toiletries. I was confused. She didn't tell me anything about going out with Kay Kay. The one Friday I come home early to chill with her, and she's going out. What type of shit is that?

"When was you gon' tell me, and where was my daughter going?" I asked.

"Well, you're usually not home this early, especially on a Friday night, which means I would have called you and told you, and OUR daughter was gonna go to my mother's house but since you're home, I thought she could stay with you." she explained.

"Let me get this straight, you run around here bitchin' and complaining that you want me home, that you need me, and that you want me to do more to help around here, and when a nigga start doing the shit so yo ass can stop nagging all the fucking time, you want to run yo ass out to a fucking bar? Am I missing something?"

"First, don't do me no fucking favors. Did I ask you to be here tonight? I said *when* I need you to, and NAGGING? Are you fucking serious right now? Since when do I nag? I don't ask your ass for nothing, I don't bitch about you going out when you want; in fact, I really don't say shit about anything you do but the one time you home and I'm going out it's a fuckin' problem, why?"

"BECAUSE I CAME HOME TO BE WITH YOU!" I shouted. She looked at me like I was crazy, then burst out laughing.

"Oh, you mad because you not getting your way? How old are you? Throwing fucking tantrums like you a fucking child."

"Oh, I'm childish now?"

Venus

"If the shoe fits." I replied. I couldn't believe this nigga was really upset because I wanted to go out. I hardly ever went anywhere.

"Fuck you Venus, ungrateful ass." he spat. *Oh no this nigga didn't!*

"WHAT? FUCK YOU? UNGRATEFUL?" I hollered. He had my blood boiling and I really wanted to reach out and touch his ass.

"You heard what the fuck I said," he blurted. Now I was really mad.

I walked over to him and slapped him so hard my hand stung.

"Don't you ever in your life call me ungrateful again. I may be a lot of things, but ungrateful is not one of them." He grabbed me roughly by my wrist like he wanted to hurt me. He leaned close to my face and looked me dead in the eyes.

"Don't you ever in your life put your fucking hands on me again, or I promise you I will"

"You ain't gon' do shit." I cut his ass off.

One thing for certain, two for sure, I would never tolerate a nigga putting his hands on me. I learned that at a young age. I snatched away from his grip and tried to storm off. He grabbed me. I tried to slap him again but he caught my hand and pushed me away, making me fall on the bed.

"STOP FUCKING PLAYING WITH ME, VENUS!" He yelled. He had a look on his face that I'd never seen before, but I wasn't about to back down. I wasn't built that way.

"FUCK YOU!" I yelled as I got up off the bed. I charged at him again but he caught me in a bear hug.

"Stop trying to fight me before I air yo lil' ass out in here." I was trying to wrestle out of his hold, swinging wildly and trying to hit him, but he was too damn strong and I got tired.

"LET ME THE FUCK GO!" I yelled, kicking my legs.

"CALM THE FUCK DOWN ACTIN' WILD AND SHIT!" he shouted. I swung backward and hit him in the face with the back of my fist. He slung me off of him and into the wall. He had his hand on my throat and his fist up as if he was about to hit me, but he caught himself and backed away from me with a look of shame on his face and anger in his eyes.

"I HATE YOU!" I screamed. My feelings were hurt and I wanted him to hurt like I was.

"YOU HATE ME? YOU HATE ME?!" he shouted and pushed me away from him. He had a scowl on his face and pain in his eyes.

"You wasn't hatin' my ass when I saved yo ass from going to jail, or when I put that nigga in a coma for yo ass. You ain't hate me when I paid for yo crackhead ass mother to go to rehab, or when I bought her a house. You don't hate me every fucking month when I pay yo mother's bills. You didn't hate me when I put your ass in this big ass house, or when I give you money to buy Louboutins or whatever the fuck you want, and you definitely don't hate me when I'm long dicking you down every fucking night. I think it's *I love you* then. Am I missing something? Fuck you talkin' 'bout you hate me? Fuck outta here with that shit." he ranted, pointing out everything that he'd done for me.

"I'M TIRED OF YOUR SHIT, ADONIS!" I yelled as I sat on the bed.

"THEN GET THE FUCK ON, VENUS!" he yelled. His words cut me deep. I felt my heart drop to my feet as he stormed out of the room. I felt like I couldn't breathe. The heaviness of my chest made my breathing labored. My heart ached, making my chest hurt. I placed my hands over my face and burst into tears.

Feeling broken, I dragged myself around the room packing my things, then I went down the hall and packed some things for Harmony. I got Harmony out of her playroom and headed for the door.

"Where the fuck you going?" Adonis asked, sitting on the sofa drinking a bottle of Remy 1738.

"I'm getting the fuck on like you said." I replied. He jumped up and came storming over, trying to snatch my bags out of my hands. We were fighting over the bags and he jacked me against the wall.

"STOP IT!" Harmony shouted with tears in her eyes.

Adonis immediately let me go and rushed over to her and started apologizing. I walked over and grabbed her by the hand, then walked out of the door.

The glass shattering against the door startled both me and Harmony. I hurried and got in my car and pulled off. Once I got down the street, I pulled over and burst into tears. I couldn't believe what just happened. I was confused and broken-hearted. I picked up the phone and called Kay Kay.

Kay Kay

As soon as I picked up the phone to call Venus, it started ringing in my hand; it was Loco. He wanted to come over tonight. As much as I wanted to hang out with my girl, I couldn't pass up the opportunity to see Loco. He was always so busy and we didn't get to spend much time together. Besides that, he put it down in the bedroom. I had never been fucked so good in my life, and I'd been with more guys than I would like to admit. I sat on the phone silently thinking if I should cancel my plans with Venus or not. Loco's voice interrupted my thoughts.

"So you gonna let me come over or what?" he asked. The sexy way he asked made the decision for me.

"Yeah, you can come," I replied. I put the phone on the table and went in the kitchen to put the Hennessy in the freezer so it could have a little chill on the way Loco liked it. I heard the phone ringing and rushed back into the living room to answer the call; it was Venus. I could have kicked myself for forgetting to call her to cancel our plans.

"Venus girl, I am so sorry but Loc—" the sounds of sniffles cut me off.

"Vee, what's wrong?" I asked.

"I left Adonis." she cried out. I was in shock. I would have never in a million years imagined her leaving him.

"Are you ok?" I asked. My heart ached for her. I knew how much she loved Adonis; something terrible must have happened.

"Venus, you want to come over? I can tell Loco to come later," I said, hoping that it would be cool with Loco.

"No, I'm good; I'm going to my mom's house." she sniffed.

"You sure? I mean you are more than welcome to come here," I assured her.

"I'm good, Kaylee" she said in a brittle voice.

"Ok, drive careful and call me."

"I will." She hung up the phone. I sat on the sofa still shocked by what I heard.

A few minutes later, Loco was ringing my door bell. When I opened the door, he was leaning against the wall looking sexy as hell. He walked straight into the kitchen and grabbed his bottle out of the freezer.

"You want a glass?" I asked as he turned the bottle up, taking a big gulp.

"What for?" he answered, then took another sip.

He snatched me up, gripping my ass in one hand as he kissed me. The taste of Hennessy mixed with weed filled my mouth as our tongues danced around.

"Damn baby, I love kissing those lips," he said, sucking on the bottom of my lip.

He sat down on the stool and motioned for me to sit up on the counter top. He poured some Hennessy on my thigh and sucked it up. I ran my fingers through his dreads. He pulled me to the edge of the counter, leaned me back, and poured some Hennessy on my stomach. As he was licking it off, my mind started drifting to Venus. I was still feeling her pain.

"What's wrong with you?" Loco asked, noticing that I wasn't responding to the things he was doing to my body.

"I'm sorry, I can't stop thinking about Adonis and Venus breaking up." I replied.

"What you mean they broke up?" he questioned with a confused look.

"I mean she said she left him, so I guess they broke up." I replied.

"Damn, ain't that some shit." He said, then started sucking on my neck.

"Aye man, if you gon' be salty all night I can go the fuck home." he barked.

"Loco, for real, I can't help it. Venus is my girl." I hopped off of the counter.

"I understand; Adonis is my nigga but they ain't got shit to do with us." He pulled me closer, but I snatched away.

"Yo, you need to kill this fucked up ass mood you in, shit. I could have went to see another bitch for all that." He grabbed the bottle and took another gulp, then he grabbed me and started sucking on my neck again.

"So is that all I am to you?" I asked with a low tone in my voice. He let me go and took a couple of steps back.

"Fuck you talkin' 'bout?" he asked, looking at me like I'm crazy.

"Is that all I am? A piece of ass?" I questioned with an attitude.

"Don't catch a fuckin' attitude with me 'cause yo girl goin' through some shit, you betta dead that shit right now." he barked.

"Answer the damn question, Orlando." I called his ass by his government. I was pissed.

"Oh, so you callin' a nigga's government now." He laughed. "Ok, real talk, you already know what this is, Kaylee. I told you I don't do the relationship shit."

"So I guess that's all I am." I tried to storm past him but he grabbed me by the arm.

"Let me show you something." He pulled out his phone and pulled up his messages. There were a bunch of texts from females.

"I could have been anywhere else tonight, but I choose to be with you." he stated as a matter of fact. I didn't give a shit though. I snatched his phone outta his hand and threw it across the room.

Loco

This bitch was crazy in her muthafuckin' head if she thought she was gonna get away with throwing my phone across the room. She already got a pass for talkin' to me sideways and shit. On everything, she was about to make me lay hands on her ass.

"Man, get yo ass over there and pick up my got damn phone. The fuck wrong with you?" I blurted, pushing her ass across the room. She really didn't understand that I don't give a fuck about shit. "Kay Kay, for real, don't make me fuck yo ass up in here." I added. She picked up my phone and put the battery back in it, and handed it to me like she had some fuckin' sense.

"Loco, get out." she said in a brittle voice. I grabbed her by her wrist and pulled her close to me.

"You know you don't want me to leave, stop playing games." I started kissing on her neck.

"Loco, stop." She protested but I wasn't tryna hear all that. I continued pulling up that lil' ass dress she had on and kissing her on her stomach.

She let out a soft moan and I knew that I wasn't going nowhere. I slid her panties down and sat her on top of the counter, grabbed my Hennessy, and poured it on her box. I slurped it up and repeated my actions. I laid her back, spread her legs, and ate the shit out of that Hennessy-flavored pussy. She started breathing heavy and gripping my dreads as she started grinding on my tongue.

"Damn Loco, I'm about to cum baby." she moaned, then I felt her juices running down my face.

I pulled her to the edge of the counter, put her legs on my shoulders, slammed into her roughly.

"FUCK!" she shouted. I pushed her legs back and started pounding into her.

"OOOWWW!" she hollered, tryna push me back.

"What I tell you 'bout all that fuckin' hollerin'? You want me to give this dick to another bitch?"

"NOOO!" she shouted.

"Then handle this shit." I gripped her by her waist and went deeper inside of her.

"Shit!" she moaned.

"You wanna be the only one getting this dick?"

"Yeeessss." she groaned.

"Then act like it." I continued my stroke until she exploded all down the counter. I stepped back and pulled her off the counter.

"I want to see those sexy ass lips around my shit." I said, stroking my shaft. She got on her knees and slid it in her mouth, I felt her teeth scrape my joint a little and I pulled back.

"Aye, if you don't suck this shit right, I'll call another bitch over here, tie you to a chair, and make you watch her suck it." She looked at me like I was crazy.

"Don't play with me, Loco." she said as she stroked my shaft with both hands. I smirked like I was joking, but for real for real I was dead ass. I had bitches that would do whatever I told them to do just to get this dick. She licked her lips and slid my dick in her mouth.

"Fuck shawty." I said. I didn't know what the fuck happened, but her head game was on point like shit. She was sucking my dick like a muthafuckin' pro. Had a nigga biting his bottom lip tryin' not to sound like a lil' bitch. I watched her make this big muthafucka disappear in her mouth and shawty ain't gag or shit. I had to grip the fuckin' counter to keep my balance. She looked up at me with those sexy ass eyes, and juicy ass lips—man, I released all my fuckin' kids down her throat.

Lying in Kay Kay's bed and stroking her hair as she slept on my chest had a nigga thinking I could see myself with a bitch like her. I didn't intimidate her lil' ass and I liked that. On the other hand, she might be damn near as crazy as I am and I might end up fuckin' her ass up. Her crazy ass might actually try to fight me though, and I ain't with that fighting shit—that's another reason why I ain't into that relationship thing. I tell you, soon as you lay the pipe down, bitches wanna try to put labels on a nigga and shit. Only labels I wear is the ones on my clothes. Kay Kay shifted and let out a cute little snore and I smiled. I never got tired of hearing the way she snored. I kissed her on the top of her head, held her tighter, closed my eyes, and listened to her cute little snores. I couldn't believe her ass had a nigga catching feelings and shit, what the fuck?

Adonis

It had been a week since Venus walked out on me and I was fucked up. I never thought that shit was that bad. I didn't mean to blow up on her like I did, and I was wrong. I was already feeling like a ticking time bomb ready to explode. That smart ass mouth of hers added to the fucked up shit that was already on my mind and set me off. I paced the floor with the phone to my ear, drinking a bottle of Grey Goose, hoping that Venus would answer the phone.

"Yes Adonis." She answered and my heart almost jumped out of my chest.

"What you doing?" I asked.

"Sitting here with Layna and Harmony, why?" she responded. She was answering like she didn't want to talk to me.

"Why you ain't been picking up the phone for me?"

"Because I don't want to talk to you." she said in a flat tone.

"What I do, Venus? Huh? What the hell did I do that was so fucking bad that you would leave me and not come back?"

"Want a list?" she answered.

"See, why the fuck you gotta always be a fuckin' smart ass all the time?"

"Ok, Adonis; first you was trippin' 'cause I wanted to go out for a little while, then you called my mother a crackhead, and on top of all that you slammed me into a wall."

"You put your hands on me first."

"Really, Adonis?" Neither one of us spoke for a few seconds. "Bye Adonis."

"Venus, wait."

"WHAT!" she shouted into the phone.

"Let me talk to my daughter." She snickered, then passed Harmony the phone.

"Hiii Daaaddy." she whined with the cutest little high-pitched voice.

"Hi baby, how you doing?" I asked, almost bursting into tears. I missed my family.

"Fine, I miss you." she said.

"Daddy miss you too. I'ma come see you tomorrow, ok?"

"Ok Daddy, I love you, muah." She blew me a kiss through the phone. A lone tear fell from my eye.

"I love you too baby, muah." She passed the phone back to Venus.

"I'ma come see her tomorrow." I told her.

"Umm hum, bye." She hung up. I sat on the sofa and took another gulp as tears filled my eyes.

My doorbell started ringing.

"Man, who the fuck at my door?" I shouted as I walked toward the door.

"Me nigga, open the fuckin' door!" Lavelle shouted from the other side of the door. I opened it.

"Nigga, you look like shit. What the fuck wrong with you?" he asked, walking through the door. I closed and locked it behind him.

"Man, I'm fucked up. You know Venus left me." I stated as I picked up my bottle and took a sip.

"You want some?" I asked, holding out the bottle offering it to Lavelle.

"Hell nah nigga, yo ass look like you ain't shower or brush yo teeth in days." he chuckled.

"Man, fuck you." I took another drink and flopped down on the sofa.

"Nigga, get yo ass up and do something with yourself. Moping around here and shit. Venus left you because yo ass was trippin', now what you gonna do to get her back?"

"I don't know, she don't even wanna talk to me." I shrugged my shoulders.

Lavelle shook his head "First nigga, gimme this shit." He snatched the bottle out of my hand. "Then you gonna go upstairs, take a fuckin' shower, and get dressed. You need to get outta this fuckin' house."

"Nah, I'm good; I don't wanna go nowhere." I laid back on the sofa.

"Nigga, if you don't get yo stupid ass up off that sofa and bring yo ass on, I'ma fuck you up myself," he said, pulling me off the sofa. I went upstairs, took a shower, and got dressed.

Sitting at the bar in Lavelle's club and taking shots of Patrón, listening to him tell me how I fucked up was blowing the shit outta me. I already knew that I fucked up and I didn't need him lecturing about shit.

"Man look, you got to learn to prioritize yo life. Look at me, I'm runnin' my club, runnin' y'all niggas, and takin' care of shit for Frank, but I make time to do what I need to do for Sieda. You don't hear her ass complaining about shit." he lectured.

"Nigga, that's 'cause she got her own shit going on." I stated.

"What the fuck you think Venus is tryna do? She want her own shit too. You think she want to depend on yo ass for the rest of her life nigga?" I was too damn drunk to deal with this shit right now. I really just wanted him to shut the fuck up.

"Aight Lavelle, I feel you, but can we talk about this shit lata? I'm tryna watch Illusion's fat ass make that ass clap."

"Muthafucka, yo ass need to be figuring out how you gon' get your girl back." Loco came over to the table, gave us both dap, and sat down.

"Nigga, where the fuck you been hiding?" he asked me, pouring a shot.

"I ain't been hiding, nigga." I said. He took his shot and poured another, sitting back in his chair with his eyes focused on Illusion, who was on the pole doing some acrobatic type shit.

"Man damn, I'll have fun fuckin' her flexible ass, shit. I'll knock that bitch's pussy out the frame." he chuckled.

"Kay Kay would fuck yo crazy ass up too." I laughed. Lavelle agreed with what I said and gave me dap.

"Shiiid, Kay Kay lil' ass know what time it is. She tried to flex on me last week I had to put her ass on the counter and give her some act right. Shiid, I put the smack down on that ass, had her ass walkin' with a serious muthafuckin' limp." he bragged, taking another shot. Lavelle burst out laughing.

"Nigga, yo ass crazy for real." he chuckled.

"I'm about to call her ass when I leave here; these bad ass bitches you got in this bitch got a nigga wantin' to break a bitch's back tonight. Go balls muthafuckin' deep tryna rip some fuckin' guts out." He laughed.

Me and Lavelle both shook our heads. I ain't gon' lie, he wasn't lying. I wish Venus was home so I could do some major damage to her insides; shit, a nigga ain't had no pussy in a week and I was about to catch blue balls and shit. A nigga was backed up like a muthafucka.

We continued choppin' it up and took shots for a little while, then I had to go relieve myself. On the way from the bathroom stumbling and shit, I bumped into this nigga and made him spill his drink on himself. This muthafucka tryna show off and shit and tried to flex on me. Little did he know, I had a lot of pent up anger inside of me and I was ready to fuck some shit up.

"Nigga, watch where the fuck you going, drunk ass mothafucka." He said with an attitude as he pushed me away.

This nigga must not know who I am, I thought. I punched his ass right in the face. He fell into the bar and I grabbed him by his throat with my left hand and pounded his face with my right. I split his shit and had his ass leakin' all over the bar top. I grabbed his head and banged it on the bar top twice before Lavelle pulled me off the nigga. I was wildin' out, tryna beat that nigga brains out; flexin' on me like I'm some bitch ass nigga, he had me fucked up.

"Yo, chill the fuck out." Lavelle said, taking me to the back with Loco following behind him.

I mugged the muthafucka I was fighting as Tito scooped his ass off of the ground and walked him out.

Lavelle took me into his office and sat me down on the sofa, then him and Loco burst out laughing.

"Yo, you beat the fuck outta that nigga." Loco laughed. Him and Lavelle gave each other dap, cracking up.

"He had that shit comin' tryna punk me like I'm some bitch ass nigga. Shiid, drunk or not, I got hands and handle myself real well." I boasted. We chilled in Lavelle's office until the club closed.

As Lavelle closed everything out, Loco went to get his car so that he could give me a ride home. We walked out of the door and Lavelle turned around to lock up. I noticed someone walking toward us. The colorful lights outside of the club were dim and made it difficult for me to see clearly, but it gave me just enough light to notice that it was the nigga.

"Yeah muthafucka, you thought this shit was over? Nah son." he said, lifting his arm. He had a gun. The nigga was so busy tryna prove that he was 'bout that life that he didn't hear or see Loco walk up behind him. He grabbed the nigga in a choke hold with one arm, lifting him off the ground as he knocked his gun outta his hand with the other, then slammed his ass on the ground. I put my foot on his throat and pressed down, cutting off his air.

"You wanna shoot me, nigga?" I asked as he struggled under my foot. The more he struggled, the harder I pressed. I watched his ass squirm for a few minutes before putting a couple of bullets in his head. Lavelle called his clean-up crew to come take care of things for us, then we sat in Loco's truck drinking while Loco smoked a blunt and waited for them to get there.

After leaving the club, we went to IHOP to eat. When we sat down to eat, Loco called Kay Kay to let her know that he would be over there after we at and he dropped me off. I couldn't help but to think about Venus and how much I missed her. I was wondering if she was missing me as much as I missed her.

The waitress came to the table and sat my meal—a T-bone steak and egg combo and some double blueberry pancakes—down in front of me. I thanked her and she smiled. Her smile reminded me of Venus. I cut off a piece of steak and took a bite. Loco started talking about tearing Kay

Kay ass up when he made it to her house and my mind drifted to Venus, wondering if she was craving my like I was craving her right now. After eating all that food, I caught the 'itis and was ready to go home and go to sleep. I had to get some rest so I could sober up to go see my baby later on. I got home at almost 6 am. I took a quick shower and went straight to sleep.

I woke up around noon, feeling lightheaded and groggy, and my bladder was full as a muthafucka. I hurried to the bathroom to relieve myself and to take care of that stale alcohol taste in my mouth. My right hand was hurting like a bitch as I was tryna brush my teeth. I looked at my knuckles that were swollen and bruised and thought about the ass whippin' I put on that nigga last night. I thought whippin' his ass was enough but this muthafucka had a death wish steppin' to me with a gun. I started laughing like shit thinking about Loco's crazy ass kissing his cross talking 'bout, "Rest in peace mothafucka," after I pulled the nigga's shit back. That nigga always kissing that damn cross. I went to the kitchen and drunk a few glasses of water tryna get rid of my slight hangover. I hopped in the shower and let the warm water soothe me. After showering, I hurried and got dressed, called Venus to let her know that I was on the way, and headed out the door.

"Nigga, yo ass alive?" Lavelle shouted into the phone. I wasn't gonna answer because I knew he was only calling to fuck with me about last night.

"Man, why the hell you yelling? Damn." I replied. His loud, deep ass voice penetrated through the phone, making my head spin.

"I know yo ass hungover like shit, all that drinking. I'm surprised you outta bed." he said.

"You know I got to go see my baby," I smirked. Just thinking about Harmony and her cute little smile warmed my heart.

"Aight nigga, call me when you leave, ok?"

"Aight."

I parked my car in Venus' mother's driveway and turned off the engine. I sat there thinking for a few minutes. I had to prepare myself for seeing Venus. I hadn't laid eyes on her in a week and I knew it was gonna drive me crazy knowing that she wasn't coming home with me. I got out of the car, walked up the walkway, and knocked on the door. Venus opened it, wearing some dark blue ripped skinny jeans and a white tank top. Her perky C-cups had a nigga wanting to suck the shit outta them. We stood in the doorway staring at each other for a few seconds. She looked like she was trying to look like she wasn't bothered by our separation, but the dark circles around her eyes gave me proof—she was just as fucked up about this shit as I was.

Venus

Adonis called and said that he was on the way. I missed him so much and was excited to see him. I hurried and took a shower. My hair was frizzy and all over my head. I wet it and let it curl up. He loved my curls. You could tell that I wasn't sleeping due to the dark circles around my eyes. I didn't want Adonis to know how bad I felt. I tried to put a little of my mother's makeup on to cover them, but it only hid them a little. I threw my dark blue ripped skinny jeans on so my round apple ass would stand out, then I threw on a form-fitting tank top so my breasts would stand at attention. I wanted him to see what he was missing. Knowing him like I did, his ass was going crazy without sex. Shit, truth was, I was too but I refused to give in to him. He needed to realize that he couldn't take me for granted.

I was putting on my lip gloss when I heard a knock on the door. Anxious to see Adonis, I rushed down the steps, skipping a few in the process. I stopped to contain my excitement before opening the door. Adonis was standing there looking sexy as hell in his True Religion jeans and a Polo shirt. I could smell his Prada cologne filling the air as I stood there looking him up and down.

"Can I come in?" he asked. His deep, sexy voice interrupted the sexual thoughts that were going through my mind. I stepped aside and allowed him to come in. I closed the door, then followed him into the living room.

"So how you been?" I asked.

"Fucked up, how you been?" he replied.

"Ok I guess." I answered. We stood in the middle of the living room trying to act like we didn't feel the awkwardness between us.

"Can a nigga at least get a hug?" I gave him a hug. He squeezed me tighter and whispered, *I miss you* in my ear. I pulled out of his embrace, then yelled upstairs for Harmony to come down to see her father.

Harmony came running down the steps yelling for her daddy. He kneeled down as she jumped into his arms. They both had big goofy-looking grins on their faces. Seeing the way Harmony's face was lit up the whole time she was playing with her daddy made me sad. I knew she missed him; I missed him too. I wanted my family back together again, but I knew that I needed to take time to get myself together. I needed to put my wants first for a change.

Adonis stayed for a couple of hours and when he was leaving, he asked me if I could walk him to the car. I slipped on my shoes and followed him out through the garage. I opened the garage door and walked him to his truck. He reached under the seat and gave me a stack of money wrapped in a rubber band.

"This should take care of y'all for a minute. If you need more, call me." he said as I put the money in my back pocket. He grabbed me by my belt loop and pulled me close to him.

"I miss you, baby. Come home with me." he said as he tried to kiss me. I moved so he couldn't.

"Oh, it's like that now?" he asked, licking his lips and teasing me. I wanted that kiss but I wasn't about to give in like that.

"Adonis stop, and I'm not going to come home. I need time to work on me." I said.

"TIME? What the fuck you mean time?" he released me from his grip. He was staring at me with a scrunched face, looking confused.

"Yes Adonis, there are things I want out of life, and I think I need to do them on my own." I spoke truthfully.

"Yo, for real Venus, don't play with me. How fuckin' long you need?" he questioned in a high-pitched tone.

"As long as it takes." I replied.

"Man, stop fuckin' playing and gimme me a kiss." He snatched me up and kissed me. I tried to push him away and this nigga bit my bottom lip.

"OW!" I shouted, pushing him away. "What's wrong with you?" I asked, checking to see if my bottom lip was bleeding. He leaned against the truck cracking up.

"Stop playing with me then," He snickered. He grabbed me and pinned me against the truck.

"Come on, one kiss." He pleaded. Looking in his eyes and being that close to him made my box tingle. I really missed his ass. My heart started pounding as he leaned in for a kiss.

I could feel his dick getting hard as our tongues danced in and out of each other's mouths. He slid his hand down my back and pulled me deeper into the kiss.

"Damn, I missed you." He whispered, nibbling on my ear. I could feel myself getting moist. I pushed him away but he picked me up and carried me to the garage.

"Put me down, Adonis." I protested, but he didn't listen. He closed the garage door and set me on top of my car. He kissed me again and started unbuttoning my pants.

"Stop Adonis." I said, grabbing his hands.

"Fuck!" he groaned. He cringed in pain and held his hand. I could see that he was in pain.

"What happened to your hand?" I asked as I grabbed it and looked at it. His knuckles were swollen and he could hardly close his hand. "Adonis, what happened?" I gave him a questioning look.

"Don't worry, I'm good." I figured that he messed up his hand doing something in the streets; he kept me outta his business. He started trying to unbutton my jeans again.

"Adonis, I said stop." I pushed him away.

"Fuck that, you got on these tight ass jeans knowing a nigga ain't had no pussy since you left." He grabbed the back of my neck and kissed me, pinning my hands behind my back with his good hand while he unbuttoned my jeans with the hurt one. He slid me off of the car and bent me over the hood.

"Damn, already wet for daddy." he avowed, entering me from behind. He reached around me and started massaging my pearl.

"Damn Adonis." I said, gripping the front of the car as his stroke got deeper.

"You betta be quiet for yo moms come out here," he whispered as he gripped my hair and pulled me backward. He sucked on my ear, making my body quiver. Being in the garage with him reminded me of the times we would sneak and have sex when my mother was passed out high. Adonis gripped me by the waist and sped up his pace. My body trembled uncontrollably.

"Tell me you love me." he whispered.

"I love youH" I whispered. He let out a moan and released inside of me.

"I'ma get you and Harmony a place to stay so you won't have to stay with yo moms." He stated reaching for my hand.

"You don't have to do that." I said.

"I know. I promised that I would take care of you, and that's what I'm gonna do." He replied as he took his ringing phone out of his pocket.

"Hold up, I have to take this." he said, answering the phone.

"Yeah Beans, what's up?" he answered.

"Nothing? Man shit, well keep looking. I know something will turn up. That nigga dirty, I can feel it," he spoke into the receiver.

"Aight, talk to you lata." He hung up the phone.

"What was that about?" I asked.

"Nothing for you to worry about, but gimme a few days and I'll find a place for you." He kissed me then left.

I stood in the driveway watching him until he was no longer in my view. I walked back into the garage and closed the garage door. I put my hand on the top of my car where we'd just fucked. I couldn't believe I'd give in to him that easy. I hoped I could get my life on track quickly, 'cause I loved Adonis and I really wanted to make it work between us. I shook my head and headed in the house.

Kay Kay

I walked into the building of the manufacturing company that was making the prototypes for our line and Venus was sitting at the table talking to Pierre, one of the owners of the factory. He'd been tryna get at Venus for a couple of months now, but she was still so hung up on Adonis that she wouldn't give him no play. Pierre was fine as hell too. He was mixed with Puerto Rican and Jamaican. He was about 6 feet tall and athletic toned with dark, curly hair that he wore in a temple-tapered curly bush. He had thick eyebrows and long, dark eyelashes that made his dark grey eyes stand out. His chin strap beard and light mustache complimented his looks very well, and on top of all that he spoke with a Jamaican accent that would make any bitch's panties wet. I swear if he wasn't after my girl and I wasn't fucking with Loco, I would be on his ass like a thirsty ass thot.

"What y'all over here giggling about?" I asked, sitting down beside Venus.

"Nothing." Venus answered, picking up a couple of fabric swatches and pinning them against the sketch of one of our dresses.

My eyes were darting back and forth between her and Pierre, watching as they traded quick glances at each other. I picked up the sketchpad and stared at both the fuchsia floral print and the white floral print fabric choices, tryna decide if I really liked those them. After thinking about it for a few minutes, I decided that they weren't the right fit.

"I think that these prints would work better with the maxi dress; this dress should be a solid color." I suggested. I picked up a few solid fabric choices and switched them with the floral, then put the floral against the maxi dress. We all took a step back, admiring the selections on the table.

"Yeah, that works better.

" Venus agreed. She collected the sketchpads and fabrics and handed them to Pierre. He winked at her, taking the sketchpad outta her hands. I saw her blush. Pierre took the sketch pad with the fabric choices to the seamstress so that she could make the pattern for them. Venus and I decided to go to Florida Avenue Grill for lunch. I sensed something between Venus and Pierre, so I decided to do a little snooping.

"So, what's going on with you and Pierre?" I asked.

"Girl nothing, he keeps asking me out, that's all." she replied in a high-pitched voice.

"Ok, whatever you say." I chuckled. She started laughing.

"Girl, you know my heart belongs to Adonis." she giggled.

"Yeah, well how's he been doing? You still fuckin' him?" I questioned.

"Actually, he's been stepping up a lot, picking Harmony up from school and everything. And to answer your nosy ass question, yes I sleep with him occasionally," she replied, grinning. "Well, what about you and Loco? That nigga got yo ass open, missing meetings, jumping through hoops of fire and shit." She started laughing at her little joke about jumping through hoops of fire. I didn't find that to be funny. Yes, I did blow off a few meetings because he either wanted to come over or he kept me up too late the night before, but she knew how to handle business. She represented our brand very well on her own.

"Girl, it is what it is. But as much as that nigga on my line tryna come see me or telling me to come over, you would think we were in a relationship. Shit, the way that nigga puts it down in the bedroom, I don't care if we ever get in a relationship, long as I can keep getting the dick." We gave each other a high five, laughing like shit at how true my statement was for both of us.

The chill of the cool, autumn breeze sent shivers through my body as soon as I opened the car door. I grabbed my black leather jacket off of the backseat and put it on. I grabbed my purse off the seat and closed the door. Venus was waiting for me at the front of the car with her folder, tapping her foot. I hit the button on my key chain to lock the door. I didn't trust these DC niggas; they would jack their own momma if they had something they wanted. Shit, I knew this one nigga that stole the 14k gold cap out of his grandmother's dentures and sold it for drugs. That was some foul ass shit. Who in the fuck does that? Better question is, who in the fuck would actually buy the shit? I hit the other button turning on my car alarm and headed for the restaurant.

We were talking as we walked down the sidewalk and Venus suddenly stopped. I kept walking until I noticed that she wasn't beside me anymore. I turned around to see where she was and she was standing at the window, staring with a disdainful look on her face. I walked over to her and looked in the window to see what she was looking at.

"OH, FUCK NO!" I shouted, staring at Adonis and Loco sitting at the table with two random ass bitches. Adonis had his arm around the bitch's neck that was sitting next to him. She had her head laid back on his arm. I was pissed and ready to go in there and fuck shit up. I looked over at Venus, who was standing there with tears filling her eyes.

"You wanna go handle shit?" I asked. She shook her head no and rushed back to the car. I dug in my purse for the keys, turned the alarm off, then unlocked the doors.

"Well, I'm going in there; I'll be right back." I said, taking off my earrings and putting them in my purse. I was preparing myself for a fight if anybody jumped, including Loco and Adonis. It was gonna be a muthafuckin' brawl in that bitch. I was pissed. My girl stayed loyal to his ass and this nigga was running around here parading some random ass bitch on his arm. As for Loco, I didn't give a fuck if we weren't in a relationship. He wasn't gon' be calling me whenever he wanted and having a bitch change plans or missing important things while he stickin' his dick in other bitches. These niggas had the game fucked up. I reached in my purse and slid my blade in my pocket just in case I had to cut a bitch or a nigga; I didn't give a fuck. I went inside the restaurant, went right up to their table, and slammed my hands down on the table startling all of them.

"What the fuck is this? Y'all niggas double dating now? I mean, what's up?" I asked, mugging Adonis and Loco. Adonis slid his arm from around the bitch, looking at Loco like he was secretly telling him to check me.

"Who the fuck is this bitch?" I asked Adonis, pointing to the girl he was sitting next to.

"Bitch, I'm his girl." she said with hella attitude.

"His girl?" I laughed. "I don't know who the fuck you are, but you betta dead that fucking attitude before you get fucked up," I continued. She had the nerve to jump up.

"Bi—" Before she could get it out, I was choking the bitch, trying my best to crush her windpipe. Adonis and Loco both pulled me off of her.

"Fuck is wrong with you, Kay Kay?" Loco asked. He was holding me from behind and I was still tryna get to the bitch. The manager walked over and asked us to leave.

"Nigga, don't you see me handling this?" Loco spat. The manager backed away. Loco put me down and turned me toward him.

"What the fuck you trippin' for?" He had a firm grip on my shoulders, slightly shaking me. I tried to knock his hand off of me.

"You and this nigga sitting here with these bitches." I blurted, pushing him away from me. He burst out laughing. I tried to punch him in his face but he caught my fist and squeezed it.

"You ain't my girl." he fumed. He let me go with a push. I was about swing on his ass but the manager asked us to leave again before he called the police. I told him I was leaving. I turned to Loco and gave him an evil look.

"Oh, it's like that?" I waited for his response with raised brows and perched lips. When he didn't respond, I nodded my head. "Ok, do you. Then pull out a chair, sit back, and watch me do the fuck out of me." I started walking away.

"Kay Kay," he called behind me. I turned around. "I'll talk to you lata," he added. I walked back toward him.

"Nigga, hell naw, I might be busy." I looked at Adonis and said, "Oh yeah Adonis, Venus is outside and she saw you." The look on his face was priceless. He looked like he'd seen a ghost. I put my middle fingers up at them both and stormed out. By the time I made it to the car, Adonis was at my heels following me to my car.

Venus

Words couldn't describe what I was feeling right now. Seeing Adonis cuddled next to that bitch had me filled with so many different emotions. I was hurt, angry, confused, and jealous all at the same time. Part of me wanted to go in there and fuck some shit up, but the other part wondered why I would go in there and make a fuckin' fool out of myself over a trifling ass nigga. It was obvious he didn't care about me. I'd been fucking him for months now even though we weren't together, and he'd never mentioned anything to me about dating anyone.

"How could he not tell me? How could he let me find out this way?"

My mind started racing and I felt as if I couldn't breathe. I placed my hands over my face, then laid them on my lap and started bawling my eyes out. I was crying so hard that I could feel the car shaking. I opened the glove compartment and grabbed a tissue. I wiped away the snot that was running out of my nose, then blew my nose. I grabbed another one to wipe away my tears. My chest was hurting. I rested my head on the head rest and took deep breaths, trying to relieve the pain but there was no way to ease my pain. I closed my eyes as tears started to fall again.

The car door suddenly opened. I didn't bother to open my eyes; I knew it was Kay Kay.

"How could he do this to me, Kay Kay?" I sobbed. I covered my face with my hands and burst into tears.

"I'm sorry." Adonis said in a quiet voice, removing my hands from my face. He wiped away my tears then pulled me into a loving embrace. I needed to be held at that moment so I buried my head in his chest and cried my heart out. He whispered *I love you* in my ear over and over, and then he started telling me how sorry he was. I became angry.

"GET THE FUCK OFF OF ME!" I yelled, pushing him away from me so hard that he stumbled backward, almost falling on the ground. I hopped out of the car quickly and started swinging on him.

"Venus, let me explain," he pleaded, holding me by the wrist so that I couldn't hit him again.

"Who the fuck is that bitch?" I asked with a scowl on my face. He didn't respond right away.

"She say she's his girlfriend," Kay Kay said from the trunk of the car.

"GIRLFRIEND?!" I screamed. With every bit of strength, I had, I snatched my right hand out of his and punched him in the chest.

"Don't hit me again, Venus." He said, pinning me against the car.

Kay Kay rounded the car and pushed him off of me. If looks could kill, Kay Kay's ass would be dead as hell. Adonis stood there breathing hard with his hands on his head trying to calm himself down.

"How long, Adonis?" I asked in a low tone.

"Two months, but it's not that serious," he stated. I snapped my head in his direction so quick I could have snapped my neck.

"TWO MONTHS, ADONIS!" I shouted. I lifted off of the car ready to swing again.

"On everything, if you hit me I will knock both of y'all asses out.

" he warned. He knew I was gonna try to knock his head off his shoulders and if I swung, Kay Kay would have swung too. That was my girl and she was 'bout that life. That's why her and Loco were perfect for each other; she was almost just as crazy as he was. I decided not to swing, of course. I folded my arms across my chest, pinning my hands down. He calmed down and began to speak.

"Look Venus, me and Raquel a—"

"Raquel? So the bitch name is Raquel?" I chuckled, cutting him off.

"Yes, but like I was saying, it's nothing—we ain't serious at all." he continued. He took a step toward me and I put my hands up to stop him from coming any closer.

"Adonis, go back in there with yo bitch and leave me the hell alone." I opened the car door and started to get in.

"What the fuck I was supposed to do, Venus? I missed you." I looked at him in disbelief.

"So you saying that you're fucking with that bitch 'cause you missed me? What type of bullshit is that? What the fuck you think I'ma do, fall into your arms and say that it's ok?" I questioned. He stood there looking dumbfounded. I shook my head, then got in the car. He tried to open the door but I had already locked it.

"Have a nice life!" I shouted out of the window as Kay Kay pulled away.

Kay Kay pulled into the gas station parking lot and parked the car. She turned toward me and asked if I was alright. I shook my head no. She unhooked her seatbelt and embraced me. She held me for a while longer, then she grabbed her phone and called Pierre. She told him that we had an emergency and wouldn't be coming back today, then she instructed him on the things we need the seamstresses to do. She got off the phone with him and turned toward me.

"We gonna go to my house and get fucked up." she told me, putting her seatbelt back on.

"No, Kaylee. I really just want to go home alone right now, just take me back to my car." I insisted. She nodded her head in agreement and took me to my car.

"What you need to do is call Pierre's fine ass and tell him you will go out with him." she chuckled.

"You a mess, girl." I giggled.

"They say the best way to get over a man is to get under a new one." She bounced her ass in her seat and started laughing. I shook my head.

"You gonna be alright?" she asked as I got outta the car.

"Yeah I'm fine, how about you, are you ok?" I asked concerned. Kay Kay was tough but I knew that she was easily hurt, and I knew how much she really liked Loco.

"Yeah girl, I'm gonna take my ass home and drink my problems away." she giggled as if she was joking, but I knew she was serious. I leaned in her window and gave her a hug and a kiss on the cheek, then hopped in my car and went home.

Loco

Adonis was acting like he was all cool and calm when Kay Kay was in here trippin', but as soon as she said that Venus saw him that nigga's heart dropped to his feet. He got up so fast and rushed outta there so fuckin' quick that he almost beat Kay Kay to the car. I rested my hand on my head trying to control my anger. One thing I hated was for a bitch to cause a fuckin' scene, especially if we weren't together in the first place. I shook my head at the thought of Kay Kay actin' all wild and crazy, then I snickered. How the fuck did my ass get caught up in all this drama? I wasn't there with that bitch. I met Adonis there to give him his shit he left in my car. The food smelled bomb and my stomach started growling like a mothafucka, so I sat my ass down to eat. I was tryna enjoy my food when Kay Kay ass came bellowing in there wildin' out. Raquel and the bitch she was with Nytashia, Nyisha, whatever the fuck the bitch name was, was sitting at the table chattin' it up. They were going on and on about how Adonis jumped for Venus and all this other shit, blowing the fuck outta me.

"Shut the fuck up." I said through clenched teeth. "That's his got damn daughter's mother. If she not good, he not good, that's how that nigga is. You deal with it or you don't. Either way, you gonna sit yo ass here and be the fuck quiet." I continued.

"You don't know me and—" Raquel thought she was about to go in on me, but I cut that bitch off.

"You don't know me either and trust me, you don't want to know me. I don't give a fuck about you or this bitch right here." I pointed at her friend. "Shut the fuck up or I promise I will shut you up." She searched my eyes and saw how serious I was. She huffed and rolled her eyes, then sat back in her chair, crossed her legs, and started bouncing them. She was obviously pissed but I didn't give a fuck.

Adonis came back in the restaurant looking like a little lost dog or something. I asked if he was alright and he nodded his head yeah. I gave him some dap and told him I was about to get outta there. He nodded his head again like he wasn't paying me no attention. I knew that nigga had some shit on his mind, so I just left him alone and headed to Kay Kay's house. I had some shit to get off my chest. I got in my whip and called Kay Kay.

"WHAT?!" she answered, shouting in the phone.

"Aye man, take that shit down a thousand." I replied as I turned the key in my ignition.

"What you want, Loco?" she asked, still giving me a funky ass attitude.

"Where you at?" I asked.

"None of your business."

I was tryna remain calm 'cause I knew she was mad. I wanted to talk to her face-to-face and explain the situation, but she was really starting to piss me off. This was the type of shit I hated in a relationship. Bitches always copped lil' shitty ass attitudes and tried to carry a nigga like I'm one of these dumb ass fuck niggas out here.

"Kay Kay, I ain't for all this, just tell me where the fuck you at so I can come holla at you." I spoke as calmly as I could.

"There's nothing to say, Loco. You doing you, right?" she asked in a sarcastic tone.

"I can find yo ass easy but I'm not tryna go through all that, so you either tell me where you are or I'ma call my boy and find out— the choice is yours." I waited for a response.

"I'm home." she said in a low voice.

I hung up the phone and headed up New York Avenue on the way to her house.

I pulled into her driveway, shut the engine down, and waited for a few minutes hoping that she didn't go the hell off and make me jack her ass up. I swear, that girl could go from 0 to 100 real quick. I think that was why my crazy ass liked her ass so much. She was damn near as crazy as I was, but what I liked the most about her was that she was not intimidated by my aggressiveness. I think that's why we matched well together. She knew how to tame me and I sho nuf knew how to tame her ass.

I knocked on the door then leaned against the wall, waiting for her to answer. She opened the door and stood in the doorway with her arms folded. I snickered and shook my head at her mad face. I thought it was the cutest face. I walked past her and headed in the kitchen. I opened the freezer.

"No Henny for me?" I asked, moving the food around and looking for a bottle of Hennessy. She usually put a bottle in the freezer to chill when she knew that I was coming over.

"Tell that bitch you was with today to put a bottle in her freezer." she snapped. I got up in her face.

"Only bitch I want is you, Kay Kay." I tried to kiss her but she moved.

"Fuck you Loco, you think I'm stupid? I saw you with that bitch, so try a new lie—lying ass nigga."

She stormed into the living room and flopped down on the sofa. I followed her and sat down beside her. She was staring up at the ceiling pouting and I had to laugh. She looked at me and rolled her eyes. I moved closer to her.

"I don't even know that bitch, she was some friend of the girl with Adonis. I went to meet him, we started talkin' and a nigga got hungry, so I sat down to eat. That's it." I explained.

"Loco, don't try that shit with me. You said I'm not your girl so fine, do you like I said." She tried her best to contain the bitterness in her voice. She was hurt and I could tell. I rubbed my hands down my face and let out a sigh. It was time for me to do something I never did before. I had to let my guards down and tell Kay Kay how I really felt about her. I turned to face her. I took her hands into mine and spoke from the heart.

"Kaylee, this shit ain't me, aight? I'm not used to expressin' my feelings and shit but you do something to a nigga, understand? This shit crazy." I stood up and started pacing the floor. She was silent but watched my every move. I hoped she would speak 'cause a nigga wasn't used to being all in his fuckin' feelings and shit. Kay Kay had me actin' like a lil' bitch ass nigga and I didn't like that shit.

"Loco, stop pacing the got damn floor. If you got something to say, spit it out; otherwise, you can leave." I looked at her like she'd lost her fuckin' mind. I was over here pacing the floor, tryna figure out the words to say so that I didn't look like a punk and she was talking shit. Sitting over there with her sexy ass legs crossed, I could see her ass cheeks peeking through her short ass shorts. Damn, she was sexy as fuck. She got up and started walking toward the door. I was about to leave. I snatched her up by her arm.

"I'm tryna tell you that I fuck with you, shawty!" I shouted. She laughed.

"Is that your way of telling me you like me?" she asked, still laughing.

"Man, kill that shit for real." She stopped laughing when she saw the seriousness on my face.

"Ok you like me, now what? You wanna relationship with me?" she questioned. She crossed her arms over her chest.

"You know how I feel about that."

"Nah nigga, we way past that shit. Either you in or you out, you make the choice."

We stared at each other for a few minutes. I was tryna figure out how the hell we got here. I had her jumpin' whenever I called, canceling meetings, changing plans, hopping outta bed in the middle of the night, and anything else just to get this dick. I thought I had her where I wanted her, but she flipped the script on my ass—she had me where she wanted me: thinking about a relationship. How the fuck did that shit happen? Fuck it, I'm a man, I can handle this shit.

"I'm in." I spoke truthfully. There was no need to fight it anymore; she had me and I had her. She smiled. I yoked her ass up by her shirt.

"You betta hold a nigga down." I said. She kissed me. This kiss was different from any other kiss we had; it was more sensual and filled with a lot more passion than usual.

"You betta hold me down or I swear I will fuck you up." she chuckled. I slid my hands down her back and gripped her ass.

"You know you in trouble, right?" I asked, walking her toward the bedroom. She had a nigga in his feelings, making me feel like a soft ass bitch. Even though I had feelings for her, I was still the same fucked ass nigga that she met; there's no bitch in me. Ain't shit changed but the relationship, and I was about to prove to her ass that I was still that nigga. I was about to knock that pussy out the frame.

I sat up in the bed and looked around bedroom at the mess we made tryna fuck each other to sleep— I won. Kay Kay was curled up with her head under the covers knocked the fuck out. I got my blunt off the table next to the bed, fired it up, and took a pull. Blowing the smoke from the loud, I started thinking about Adonis. He loved Venus, no doubt, but the nigga's mind was fucked up sometimes. I shook my head and took another pull of the loud. Raquel was supposed to be a piece of pussy, that's it and that's all; but this muthafucka was actin' like he was tryna wife the bitch. Type of fuck boy shit was that? He wasn't no fuck boy by a long shot, but I didn't know what was up with him. I knew he had betta man the fuck up before he lost Venus—if he hadn't already.

"Let me hit that." Kay Kay said in a low, groggy voice as she stretched.

"Since when you start smoking?" I was curious. She never asked to smoke. She sat up, ran her fingers through her *I just got the shit fucked outta me* hair, then reached for my blunt.

"I just wanna try it." she chuckled.

"Shid, you already high from this dick, you don't need nothing else." I joked.

"Shut up and pass me the jay." she laughed. I passed it to her. She took a pull and started choking like she was dying. I laughed like shit.

"How the fuck you smoke that shit?" she coughed.

"Gimme my shit, wasting good weed—the fuck wrong with you?" She laid her head me as I took another pull and then I kissed her, blowing the smoke in her mouth. She started coughing again.

Adonis

I couldn't believe Venus saw that shit after all the begging she made me do to get her ass to agree to work on our relationship. A nigga had to do some Keith Sweat crying and begging shit, but baby girl finally came around. The day she saw me at Florida Avenue Grill with Raquel fucked our shit all up, and now she wouldn't even talk to me. I knew she was hurt. Seeing her sitting in the car crying her eyes out broke my heart, but knowing I was the reason she was so hurt crushed me. I didn't think there was any coming back from that; she won't be able to forget what she saw. My ass was on some real-live, cuddle type shit, doing the whole PDA and shit. The fucked up thing about that was this shit with Raquel was never supposed to go that far. I was supposed to fuck that bitch and send her ass on her way. Shit went all the way left. The bitch kept calling me and begging to see me, and Venus was on some ole *we can't keep fuckin' all the time* shit. Next thing I knew, this bitch talking 'bout she was my girl. Now that Venus wasn't fucking with a nigga, I let that bitch believe that shit. Shit, it was better than not having nobody but no matter what I did with these hoes out here, Venus would always be my baby.

"Nigga, are you fuckin' paying attention?" Lavelle's loud thunderous voice interrupted my thoughts.

"My bad, Lavelle." I apologized.

"My bad? I'm talking business and yo ass sitting over there staring into space and shit, what the fuck you thinking about?" he asked. I gave him the *you already know* look. He shook his head.

"Nigga, I have more important shit to worry about. You fucked up. I told you not to fuck with that bitch; you ain't wanna listen to a nigga. This all on you, my nigga. I got money coming up short and shit and you sitting in here looking all stupid 'cause you fucking yo shit up." he ranted. He rubbed his hand across his beard before continuing. "So, you niggas think this is a fucking game? We just handled one situation and now this shit. I tell you what, this better be the last fucking time my shit come up missing or short. Y'all niggas betta be on your shit, have yo fucking team in check. This shit is embarrassing. I gotta take this shit to Frank, making me look like I can't run my own fucking team. You niggas keep fucking playing with me and you won't have a fuckin' team. I'll run all this shit by my damn self, try me. Y'all should be on y'all team, making sure yo shit is in order for real for real. Money outta my pocket is money outta your pockets."

He stood behind his desk with a scowl on his face as his rage-filled eyes darted back and forth from me to

Maurice. He walked over to his mini-bar, poured himself a drink, then went back to his desk and sat down. You could feel the tension in the air as Lavelle's stress level elevated. He took a shot of Patrón then rubbed his tapered beard.

"Maurice, this was the merch from your deal, right?" he asked in a toneless voice.

"Nah, it was Adonis' territory." he answered. I couldn't believe that punk muthafucka tried to throw me under the fuckin' bus. I ain't have shit to do with the fuckin' deal.

"What nigga? He talkin' about the deal, not the fuckin' territory. The fuck you tryna say, muthafucka?"

"I'm saying, maybe you need to watch what the fuck your little runners doin', nigga." he replied. I knew this nigga wasn't tryna flex on me today. I already didn't fuck with him and he wanted to come at me on some bullshit.

"Maybe he should watch yo ass, grimy ass bitch." I spat. This bitch ass nigga had the muthafuckin' balls to jump. I caught his ass with a quick right to his face. I tried to knock that nigga's head off. He stumbled back, checked his nose for blood, then charged at me. We were fighting all through Lavelle's office, breaking shit and tearing shit up. I had the nigga on the ground. I wanted to stomp a mud hole in his bitch ass but Lavelle stopped it.

POW! POW!

Lavelle sent two warning shots in the air, getting our attention.

"You bitches done giving love taps and shit? You wanna be mad now, yo asses should've been mad when my fuckin' money came up short. Sit y'all bitch asses down somewhere and act civilized before I pull both of y'all niggas' shit back." He sat back down in his chair, put his gun on the desk, and lit a cigar.

"Maurice, Adonis was right. You the one handling the deal, and shit ain't adding up to what was quoted to me. If they don't have the merch, then the money can't be made. I need you to check that shit with Rojas to make sure shit is adding up on your end." he told him.

"Aight, boss." Maurice responded.

"And Adonis, get outta your fuckin' head and get back to business. How the fuck you gonna run yo shit right if you ain't right? Check with your runners in your territory and make sure their shit is adding up. Money is coming up short from somewhere and y'all niggas betta find it and handle it." he ordered.

Lavelle dismissed Maurice. I stayed behind to talk to the nigga before leaving to take Raquel to dinner.

"So you gon' shoot me, nigga?" I asked laughing.

"Man fuck that, fuck wrong with you in here fighting and shit?" he asked.

"I told you Lavelle, that nigga grimy. Watch him, he gon' try to throw my ass in that shit. I know my money's right." I replied.

"Yo man, chill with Maurice nigga, I keep telling you that shit."

"Fuck that nigga, he lucky I ain't murk his bitch ass in here."

"Nigga, chill the fuck out," he chuckled. "What the hell you getting in tonight?" he asked.

"Shit, Raquel wanna go to Ristorante Tosca, that lil' Italian joint on F Street" I answered.

"Oh yeah, I know the spot. Me and Sieda went there a few times, that shit is bomb."

"Yeah, she been trippin' 'bout me not taking her out and shit so I'ma take her to shut her ass up. Shit since that day Venus saw us, the bitch been talkin' 'bout she love a nigga and all that bullshit—man, fuck that, I love no hoe.'"

"Nigga, get the fuck outta here." he laughed. I gave him dap and walked out of the door.

I got in my car and immediately called Beans. I needed to see if his niggas on the streets could find out about this deal with Rojas. The way Maurice quickly tried to take the attention off of him and that deal and turn it on me only heightened my suspicions about his snake ass.

"Beans." he answered.

"What's up nigga, I need another favor." I stressed.

"What, you ain't talking shit? This must be serious." he stated.

"I need your best informant on this. I need to find out all I can about the deal Maurice made with Rojas."

"On it, I know just the niggas to put on the streets." As soon as I hung up, Raquel called to make sure I was on the way home to shower and change so we could go eat.

Walking into Tosca's was like walking inside of one those fancy restaurants that corporate CEOs took their potential clients to when they were trying to impress them. With its neutral stone and champagne-colored tones accented with natural wood, rich fabrics, and spectacular glass wine displays, the environment was sleek and luxurious. The server, dressed in a formal jacket, led us to our table and went about his duties with eloquence.

"Adonis, how nice is this?" Raquel asked with a big grin on her face.

"It's nice, Raquel." I answered, looking through the menu.

The server came back to the table and asked if we were ready to order. I nodded my head yes, then ordered a bottle of 1964 Cabernet Sauvignon for the table and Spaghetti Gragnano, which was spaghetti with shrimp, mussels, clams, and scallops in a spicy tomato sauce. I also ordered a prime New York strip loin in a mushroom-brandy sauce. Raquel ordered a Zuppa salad, which was chilled, yellow tomato soup, crab meat, garlic, croutons, and a roasted halibut with shallots in a fennel-artichoke sauce. A few minutes after ordering, the server came back to the table with the chilled bottle of wine and filled our glasses. We thanked him and he walked away.

Raquel was sitting at the table running her mouth about shit that I wasn't interested in. I was pretending to listen, but my mind was on business. I needed to set up a meeting with my workers just to make sure my shit was straight. I didn't want none of this shit coming my way. I didn't know what the fuck was up with Maurice, but that shit he'd pulled today had a motive behind it and I intended on finding out what it was. The server came to the table with our food.

"This looks so good." Raquel exclaimed as the server sat her food in front of her. I nodded my head in agreement as I took a sip of my wine.

I was enjoying my meal and half-way listening to Raquel when I heard a giggle that I knew all too well. I looked up from my plate and laid eyes on Venus. She was walking to a table holding on to some mixed-looking nigga's arm, giggling and shit. My blood instantly began to boil. I was ready to fuck something up. They sat down as the server passed them their menus. I sat and watched while this nigga made my woman laugh. I watched her twirl her hair with her finger and slightly tilt her head. The server came back with their food. It looked like she ordered the same spaghetti that I was having and I smiled. This bitch-made nigga made a toast and I could feel rage shoot through my body. The way I was feeling watching her with this nigga made me imagine what it must have felt like for her seeing me with Raquel. Seeing her with another nigga had me sitting at the table of Ristorante Tosca pissed the fuck off, but knowing that I was the reason she was with him and not me was fucking me up inside. I let the life that I live come between the life that I created with her. She was the love of my life and still I loved her like shit. I believed she still loved me too, but for some reason we couldn't seem to get this shit right. If losing her taught me nothing else, it taught me that love was never enough. She never complained about how I got my money or complained about me not being home. All she wanted was for me to be there when she needed me and I couldn't do that.

I sat back in my chair as I watched them sitting in the booth in this restaurant having what seemed to be a romantic dinner. I watched her shake her head, touching his arm and laughing as if he was amusing. She smiled at him the same way she used to smile at me. I could feel anger mixed with jealousy building in my body. Her beautiful oval-shaped amber eyes sparkled with joy as she giggled with a slight snort. My heart dropped; I loved that giggle. I missed that giggle.

"Adonis, do you hear me?" Raquel asked, snapping her fingers to get my attention.

"What you say?" I asked with frowned brows.

"I said Venus looks happy, don't she? It's good that she's found someone," she said with a smile. Her tone was filled with excitement, not because she was happy for Venus like she said, but because she was getting a thrill out of rubbing it in my face. She knew that being happy for Venus was the last thing I was feeling. I was mad as hell. I wanted to go over there and put a bullet in the nigga's head and claim what was mine. I picked up my drink and took a sip, still staring at Venus. Raquel was looking at me with a scowl.

Her arms were folded her across her chest, and her lips were perched.

"Maybe we should go speak." she said as she started to stand up.

"Raquel, sit yo ass down." I demanded.

"Why we can't go speak?" she asked, giving me a questioning look.

"Because I said we not." I spat.

"Well, you haven't taken your eyes off of her since she walked in the door. You sure you don't wanna speak?" Her sarcastic tone was adding fuel to the fire and I was about ten seconds from exploding on her ass.

"Don't start this shit, Raquel." I warned her.

"Why, because it's her, your precious Venus?" she questioned. I wanted to reach across the table and slap her ass. "Here I am, sitting across the table staring at the man that I love while he's staring at another bitch. What the hell is wrong with that picture?" she added.

"Raquel, shut the fuck up. I'm warning you, don't call her a bitch." I said, gritting my teeth.

"Really, you defending her over me?" she smirked. "You sitting over here looking like you could kill a nigga because that bi—oh excuse me, you warned me— because she came prancing her ass in here with another nigga on her arm." She rolled her eyes, then gave me a blank stare.

"Your point?" I asked, giving her the same blank expression that she was giving me.

"My point is I'M your fucking woman." she said with a slightly raised voice. She closed her eyes tightly and took a deep breath. Her face was tense and her nose was flaring out and in whenever she breathed.

"You disrespecting me because of her, and she hasn't looked this way once." she pointed out. Her voice was taut as she continued in a low tone, clenching her teeth. "You still love her, don't you?"

"Shut the fuck up, Raquel." I spat.

"Look how you talking to me because of her. It's always about her, so admit it Adonis, you love her." she said as she sat back in her seat and crossed her legs

"I'm not having this conversation with you." I gave her an evil look.

"It's no conversation, just answer my damn question." She squinted her eyes to show her anger.

"Alright, you want me to admit it, FINE. I LOVE HER, OK?" My voice carried through the restaurant getting everyone's attention—including Venus', who was staring at me wide-eyed with her mouth wide open, holding her chest like she was clutching her pearls. That nigga she was with must have noticed the look on her face too because he slowly turned his head in the direction she was looking. I saw him mugging me out of the corner of my eye. Usually, I would have fucked his ass up, but right now my attention was on Venus.

Raquel had her hand over her mouth and tears in her eyes staring at me. She blinked and a tear fell. She wiped the tear from her eye then threw her napkin on the table, her drink in my face, and stormed out of the restaurant. I picked up my napkin and wiped my face, then placed $200 on the table and headed out of the restaurant. As I was walking past, Venus grabbed my wrist, stopping me in my tracks. There were no need for words spoken or glances exchanged. The tension between the two of us spoke volumes. I stood there with her holding my wrist for a brief moment. I wanted to look her in her eyes so she could see that I meant what I said in my outburst. At the same time, I felt that I may have caused enough problems for her. I felt her hand suddenly release my wrist. I let out the breath that I wasn't aware that I was holding, then walked away.

Venus

My first and last date with Pierre was a disaster. Adonis was there with his bitch Raquel. I was having so much fun with Pierre that I didn't see them sitting a few tables away. It wasn't until I heard him shout that I even noticed him. I looked up and he was staring directly at me. I was shocked. I sat at the table staring at him wide-eyed, my mouth open and my hand on my chest. Pierre looked at me, then at Adonis and gave him a mean mug. I knew that it was about to be some shit. Usually, Adonis would have fucked him up for that, but he didn't. In fact, he never took his eyes off of me. Everyone in the restaurant was watching us as if we were putting on a show for them, which would have normally embarrassed the shit out of me but not this time. This time, I was flattered. I loved Adonis and I would always love him. It was no secret that he still loved me as much as he flirted with me, but there was something about the way he said it, like it almost hurt him to say it. His eyes had both love and pain in them and as he stared at me, he solidified it. My heart started pounding.

Raquel stormed out of the restaurant then Adonis put some money on the table and followed her. As he was walking by, I grabbed his wrist to stop him. I wanted to say something, but the words wouldn't escape my mouth. I felt drawn to him, like a moth to a flame, and I could tell he felt it too. Neither one of us could look at the other, afraid that our eyes would convey the message of deep love that neither one of us could deny. As much as it killed me, I had to let him go. My heart dropped as he walked out of the door.

"Who was that?" Pierre asked angrily.

"My daughter's father." I replied. The tension between me and him was so thick that you couldn't cut through it with the sharpest knife.

"You still love that nigga?" he spoke to me in a disrespectful tone. I ignored it because I understood that he felt disrespected as well. I placed my hands over my face and took a deep breath as I ran them down my face.

"Yes, I do." I admitted, looking him in his eyes so he would know I was speaking the truth.

"You need to deal with that before making a nigga think he has a chance with you." He got up from the table and leaned over me. "Find your way home and make sure you lose my number." He walked off and left me sitting at the table alone. This nigga didn't even leave any money to pay at least his half of the bill. After paying the bill, I called an Uber.

Adonis was sitting on my steps waiting, looking distressed. I walked up the walkway and stood in front of him. We were silent for a moment, then I asked him what he was doing there.

"What? That nigga couldn't bring you home?" he asked as he stood up.

"Adonis, I'm not in the mood for your attitude, just answer the damn question."

"Who the fuck was that nigga, and when did y'all start dating?" he questioned. I couldn't believe that he was actually pissed off but I wasn't about to entertain his nasty ass attitude.

"Bye, Adonis." I pushed past him to go inside the house. Knowing him like I did, he wasn't about to leave. He followed me up the steps. I opened the door and tried to close it in his face, but he pushed it open and came storming in my house.

"Answer my fuckin' question, Venus; who the fuck was that nigga?"

"I'm not answering a muthafuckin' thing. Wasn't you sitting at the table with YOUR girl or am I mistaken?"

"Venus, I'm not playing games with you." he barked.

"Good, then leave because I'm not playing with your ass either. You got some nerve pulling a stunt like you did at the restaurant, then coming in my house asking me fucking questions like I owe you a fucking answer. Get the fuck outta here with that."

"Where's my daughter?" he asked. I burst out laughing.

"Really, are you serious right now?" I questioned with a scrunched up face.

"Dead ass." he replied.

"Adonis, go home to your girl and leave me the hell alone." I said. I wasn't about to stand there and argue with him any longer. He grabbed me by the arm and pulled me close to him.

"Don't play these fuckin' games with me, Venus," he stated through clenched teeth.

"Get the fuck off of me," I shouted, snatching away from him. "Get out, Adonis," I added in a low tone.

"I'm not going anywhere." He walked over to me, grabbed me, and kissed me. I tried fighting it but feeling his tongue swirling around my mouth awakened feelings in me that I thought I'd locked away.

"Tell me you still love me." he said in a low tone, almost like a whisper.

"Adonis, please go home to Raquel." I begged, hoping he would leave but knowing he wouldn't.

He backed me against the wall and kissed me as he slid his hands up my dress.

"You give that nigga my pussy?" he asked, grabbing me by my throat. He bit down on my neck, then sucked on it.

"No." I whispered, wrapping my arms around his neck. He kissed me again as he gripped a handful of my ass, then he slid his hand around to my box.

"You betta not have." he whispered in my ear as he sucked on my ear lobe.

As bad as I wanted him, I knew that if I had sex with him that he would think that he could do it whenever he wanted, like he owned me. I felt his erection poking me as he continued sucking on my neck. I shoved him away from me as hard as I could. He tried to grab me again but I quickly moved away. I darted to the door and opened it.

"So you don't want me no more?" he asked.

"I want you to leave. You know the saying, you ain't got to go home but you got to get the hell outta here."

"Let me stay." he said, walking toward me.

"Bye, Adonis." I responded in a serious tone. He looked me up and down with lust in his eyes, sending chills down my spine.

"I'll go now, but you already know I'll be back soon, my love."

He ran his finger down my nose, then cupped my chin. He kissed me softly on the lips then walked out of the door. I slammed the door and quickly locked it. I leaned against the door fanning myself. He had me burning with desire and I couldn't deny that. If he would have stayed a few minutes longer, I would have given into his demands and he knew that.

The ringing of my doorbell startled me; I was hesitant to open it. I knew it was Adonis. I yelled through the door asking him what he wanted. He said that he had something to give me. Thinking that he was going to give me money as usual, I opened the door. Adonis snatched me in his arms.

"You thought I was really gonna leave?" he asked, grabbing the back of my neck and kissing me passionately as he backed me into the house, closing his door with his foot. I tried resisting at first, but I couldn't fight it any longer.

"Adonis, why are you doing this to me?" I whispered as he sucked on my neck.

"Because I love you, and I want you." he answered as he slid his hands under my dress. He picked me up and I wrapped my legs around his waist, and my arms around his neck.

"I love you, too." I said in a low tone as he carried me to my bedroom.

After everything that transpired between me and Adonis, I couldn't believe I was waking up in his arms again. I couldn't believe I had sex with him again. I stroked his cheek, then kissed him softly on the lips to wake him up. He didn't move. I sucked his bottom lip in my mouth. He grabbed the back of my head, pulling on top of him as he kissed me. Sliding his hands down my back and gripping my ass, he pulled me up and deeper into the kiss.

"Damn, you must really love a nigga kissing me like that with morning breath." he chuckled.

"You must love me too 'cause you kissing me with morning breath." I gave him a quick peck.

"I do love you—morning breath and all." He brushed my hair from my face and kissed me again.

Adonis

Pulling the covers over my head, I rolled over tryna escape the bright sunlight that was beaming through the window. It was too damn early to be up on a fuckin' Saturday. I was still tired as hell from Friday. I spent most of the day checking on my traps and my workers. The shit with the money coming up short had a nigga trippin. Something just wasn't adding up for me. I knew the amount of merch that I supplied to my traps, how much each product cost Frank, and how much we could make off each product and the profit wasn't there. It was like we were pushing weight and the shit wasn't paying off.

After checking on my shit, I met Lavelle at the bar for drinks and to discuss business. We both thought that the problem with the money was coming from the deal with Rojas. Lavelle thought Rojas was tryna cheat Frank and I thought Maurice fucked up somewhere, as usual. We decided to agree to disagree. I got tired of that nigga defending Maurice. I knew he was Frank's son and he'd known this nigga all his life, but fuck that—he needed to trust what I was telling him. I was starting to feel like the nigga didn't trust my ass.

I left the bar around 10 pm with a nice ass buzz and decided to stop by Venus' house, where I stayed until the wee hours in the morning. We'd been fuckin' around again for the last two months. She wanted me to leave Raquel and was tryna be patient with me, but my ass had been procrastinating like shit. I really didn't give a fuck about Raquel, but at the same time I really didn't want to hurt her. I knew that shit sounded fucked up but it was what it was. I knew I had to man the fuck up and do it soon before Venus left my ass alone.

I heard music blasting from the bathroom. I put the pillow on top of my head to block out the sound, but it didn't work. Knowing that there was no way I would be able to get back to sleep with Raquel making all that damn noise, I sat up in bed yawning and stretching, tryna wake the fuck up. I picked up my cell and saw a text from Venus.

I need you to come over, we need to talk.

Shit like that could really fuck with a nigga's head. What the fuck we need to talk about? Knowing Venus, it could be a lot of things but I wasn't about to sit here and wrack my brain tryna figure out what she wanted to talk about. I scrolled down my contact list and found her name. I listened to make sure I still heard Raquel singing in the shower. She sounded terrible and I wished she would shut the fuck up. I pushed talk and waited for the phone to connect the call.

"Hey Adonis," she answered with a brittle voice.

"What's wrong?" I asked as I hopped up outta bed quickly. It was like her voice put a nigga on high alert.

"Nothing is wrong, I'm just not feeling well. Can you come by, I need to talk to you?" she asked. I was a little calmer.

"Yeah, I'ma hop in the shower and be on my way. You need anything?"

"No, I'm good."

"Aight, I'll be there shortly."

I tossed the phone on the bed and rushed to my closet to find something to throw on. I decided to wear grey sweatpants and a white tee. I grabbed my grey and white Jordan retro 12s out of the box and placed everything on the bed.

Raquel was coming out of the bathroom as I was getting my boxers, beater, and socks out of the dresser drawer.

"Adonis, I need to talk to you." she said.

"I don't have time, I will holla at you lata when I come home." I replied, rushing into the bathroom to shower. I quickly showered, then got dressed. Raquel was on the phone running her mouth as usual. Without saying a word, I grabbed my keys and headed out of the door.

Venus opened the door wearing some lil' ass pajama shorts and a tank top, looking sexy as fuck. The way her lil' apple ass was jiggling in those shorts had a nigga dick tryna get hard. She went into the living room, laid down on the sofa, and pulled her Washington Redskin's throw blanket over her legs.

"What's up Venus, you ok?" I asked, sitting next to her and placing her legs on my lap. She scooted up so that she was sitting with her back against the arm of the sofa.

"I've been feeling sick lately and I'm late." she stated. I was confused at first, then I realized what she was telling me.

"Are you saying you're pregnant?" I asked, just to be sure. She covered her face with her hands and took a deep breath before nodding yes.

I was shocked, but excited—no actually, I was thrilled. I moved closer to her and yanked her up in an embrace, rocking her from side-to-side. She started laughing.

"Adonis, I don't know yet; I haven't taken the test." She chuckled as I buried her head in my chest.

"Well, what are you waiting for?" I asked in a high-pitched tone, not being able to contain my excitement.

"I was waiting on you. I wanted to take it with you." she snickered. She reached under the pillow that she was laying on and pulled out an unopened First Response home pregnancy test. I hopped up off the sofa, making her tumble over and catching her before she could fall.

"My bad, baby." I apologized as I lifted her to her feet and rushed her to the bathroom.

My hand was trembling as I fumbled to open the box. Venus was sitting on the toilet trying not to laugh, but of course she couldn't contain it.

"Damn Adonis, slow down. You more excited now than you was when we was taking the test when I was pregnant with Harmony." she giggled her little cute snorting giggle.

"Man, I was 17, I wasn't excited." I chuckled as I finally got the box opened and passed her the test.

Checking the time on my watch, I started thinking about how long three minutes seemed when you were waiting for pregnancy test results. When we were waiting to find out if she was pregnant with Harmony, my ass was sweating like shit, then I was really hoping that she wasn't, but this time was different. This time, I was more anxious than nervous. I wanted her to be pregnant. The joy Harmony brought into our lives was unbelievable and the love I had for her was unexplainable. I always wanted another child to bring more of those feelings in my life. I wanted me and

Venus to have the perfect little family and this baby, if there was one, could be all we needed to put us back on the right path.

Two pink lines appeared on the test. Venus looked at me wide-eyed as she shook the test as if it was gonna make the lines change. She shook it a couple more times.

"Two lines still. I'm pregnant!" she announced as she held the test out so that I could see the two pink lines clearer.

I took the test out of her hands and looked at it, then stumbled. I was so fucking happy I almost fell out. I grabbed her up in my arms and kissed her. As our tongues danced around each other's mouths, I couldn't help but to think of marriage. I already knew that I loved her and wanted to be with her for the rest of my life, so I couldn't think of any other reason why I shouldn't make it official. I couldn't stop smiling walking back into the living room and sitting on the sofa. Venus sat down against the arm of the sofa with her legs folded under her.

"So, what are we gonna do about this situation?" she asked with folded arms and a questioning look on her face.

"What? We keeping the baby, what the fuck you think?" I responded with a perplexed look on my face. I knew her ass wasn't about to sit here and tell me she didn't want my seed, fuck that.

"Adonis, of course I'm keeping this baby." She looked at me like I lost my damn mind. "Nigga, I'm talkin' 'bout the situation with your bitch. I'm not about to continue to be yo side chick. You got me fucked up, shit. I don't believe I went from a main chick to a side chick any fuckin' way."

"Venus, you not my side chick, stop fuckin' saying that shit." I grabbed her by her shoulders, giving her a little shake. "We gonna have a baby. I gotta handle a few things, then I am going home and telling Raquel that it's over, and me and you gon' do this shit right. Ain't no more separation or nothing. Either you coming home, or I'm coming here, or fuck it—we gon' buy a new house. I don't give a fuck as long, as we are together. You feel me?"

"Ok, Adonis. Do what you gotta do, but if you fuck this shit up, there ain't no coming back. I'm having this baby with or without you." she stated. I gave her my word, kissed her, and headed out of the door smiling like I had just received the greatest gift in the world—the gift that I always wanted. In reality, I did.

As soon as I got in the car, Lavelle was calling. I took a few breaths to calm my excitement. I didn't want to tell him about Venus' pregnancy yet but as excited as I was, I would have blurted it out anyway. I let his call go to voicemail. That was the only way I could avoid telling him the news. The phone buzzed immediately after it stopped ringing, alerting me that I had a text. It was from Lavelle reminding me that we were going to my mom's house the next day for dinner. I shot him a quick response: "I know." I then tossed my phone back on the passenger seat. I heard the start of Jodeci's "Forever My Lady" blaring softly through my speakers. It was on point like shit. The perfect song for the perfect moment. I turned the volume up as loud as I could stand it, and starting singing like I was K-Ci and Jo Jo wrapped in one.

After handling a couple of things at the trap, I went to Shad, my jeweler, to go ring shopping. I gave Venus my word that we were gonna do this shit right, and I intended to do that later on tonight. After spending a few hours searching through all the rings, I finally picked out one that symbolized our journey. I got her a 3-carat, emerald cut, platinum past, present, and future engagement ring. Venus was my past, my present, and my future. Shad placed the ring in a velvet heart-shaped box and put it in a small bag. He wished me good luck as he passed the bag to me. I thanked him and rushed out the store, heading home to finally end my relationship with Raquel.

I pulled up in the driveway and shut my engine off. I sat in the car for a while tryna to figure out what to say to Raquel. I didn't want to give her the normal *it's not you it's me* speech, even though it was the truth. She was a good girl, just not good enough for me. Finally deciding to just be truthful, I got out the car, put Venus's ring in my pocket, and headed in the house to give Raquel the break-up speech that was long overdue. Shit never fucking went the way you planned. This was some fucking bullshit. As soon as I walked in the door, Raquel was waiting for me.

"We need to talk." she said in a serious tone.

"Yeah we do." I replied just as serious. "You go first," I insisted, sitting on the sofa.

"Well, I been wanting to tell you this for a few days but I was afraid of how you were going to respond. I mean, we haven't really known each other that long and I..." she paused. I laid my head on the back of the sofa, hoping she wasn't tryna tell me what I was thinking she was tryna tell me and as much as I didn't want to hear those fucking words, I needed to hear them.

"Adonis, I'm pregnant." she announced.

"FUCK!" I shouted.

I woke up the next morning praying that yesterday was all a dream, but laying here staring at the engagement ring that I was twirling in my fingers was proof enough that it was real. I was fucked up. There's no way Venus was gonna accept my proposal knowing that this bitch was having my baby too. I put the engagement ring in the box, placed it in the lock box, then slid it under the bed. I rubbed my hands over my head then picked up the phone. I unlocked it and scrolled through the text messages that Venus sent this morning asking if I did what I had to do. I didn't know how to respond. I couldn't tell her the truth, but I didn't want to lie either. I placed the phone back on the table next to me and let out a loud sigh.

My phone vibrated and Lavelle's picture flashed across the screen. I knew he was calling because we are supposed to go to Mom's today but with the bullshit I just got myself into, I didn't feel like being around them. I ignored the call and the nigga called back, but I let it go to voice mail. Like clockwork, the nigga called back. I was pissed that he was ringing my line like that. I snatched the phone off the table and pressed the answer button.

Lavelle

I hadn't seen or heard from Adonis all day and it was pissing me the fuck off. He knew that today was the day we were supposed to go to Mom's house. I looked at the time and shook my head. It was going on 2 pm and we had to be at Mom's at 3:00. He knew how I hated being late. He was supposed to meet me here no later than 1:30pm. Deciding to give him a call, I picked up the phone and scrolled to his number. I put the phone on speaker while I grabbed a few things from my desk drawer. He didn't answer. I called back, but still no answer. I called back. I couldn't believe this nigga wasn't answering his phone knowing what we were supposed to do. He still didn't answer. I wasn't about to let the nigga disappoint Moms. I sat back in my chair and called the nigga again.

"Yeah nigga." he answered with bass in his voice as if he had an attitude.

"Muthafucka, why you got me ringing yo line back to back like a thirsty ass thot. You know what time it is?" I questioned with more bass in my voice that him.

"Yeah, I know." he answered nonchalantly. "I'm not going to Moms today," he added.

"Yes the fuck you is!" I exclaimed. "Nigga, I don't give a fuck what's going on with yo ass but I know one thing, we been so busy with all this bullshit going on that we haven't been keeping up with our day with ma. We promised her that we were coming and we are gonna be there, so get the fuck up and get dressed. You going even if I have to drag yo ass out the door. Remember I'm the oldest, and I will fuck you up."

"Why the fuck you always gotta play the damn oldest card?" he asked.

"Nigga I'll play the oldest card, the daddy, and any other got damn card I got to play. Get the fuck up and get dressed, I'll be there in twenty minutes."

I hung the phone up on his ass. I had to let him know that I wasn't playing with his ass and when I get to his house, he betta be dressed or I was gon' knock his lil' ass out. I was tired of playing with his ass. Nigga thought 'cause he fucked up niggas and bodied some muthafuckas that a nigga wouldn't get up in his shit. He had me fucked up and if his ass was not ready, I was gonna prove my fuckin' point.

Halfway to Adonis' house, my phone started ringing. I turned down the volume on my stereo, hit the button on my Bluetooth, and answered the call. It was Frank.

"Lavelle, I need to see you in my office at my house now." he ordered, with a loud, thunderous tone. I looked at the phone with a scrunched face, wondering who the fuck he was talking to like that.

"Frank, this can't wait? You know I don't do business when I'm spending time with my family." I snapped. I was pissed and had no problem showing it.

"No, I need to talk you now." he spoke in an emotionless tone. I agreed, then hung up the phone. I took the next exit off the beltway. I shot Adonis a quick text letting him know that I was going to see Frank first, then I called Moms to let her know that we were gonna be late. I took the exit that took me back to the beltway going south and headed to Frank's house.

I walked into Frank's office and closed the Cherrywood, soundproof door. He was sitting at his desk with a cold stare. I sat across from him waiting to hear what the fuck was so important for him to disturb me on my family day. He folded his hands under his chin and gave me a blank stare.

"You needed me?" I asked. He was looking at me as if I was a fucking stranger.

"Yeah, I need to talk to you." he stated in flat voice.

"Frank, you know that I don't do business when I'm with my family. What the fuck is so important that it couldn't wait to later?" I asked, tryna be calm. Me and Frank had kind of like a father-son relationship since he raised me in this street game. He knew that I had no problem speaking my mind.

"Lavelle, you don't walk in a man's home talking to him with disrespect." He spoke to me like he didn't know who I was. I had to take a step back and look at this nigga like he was crazy, talking to me like he didn't know who the fuck I was. Boss or not, he wasn't gon' trip on me 'cause shit was fucked up right now.

"Frank, I know you maybe fucked up over your money coming up short again, but on some real grown-man shit, don't fuckin' talk down to me. Just like you, I'm not too fond of disrespect either." I had to get his ass right. I more than likely wouldn't have said that shit in front of anyone else but in private, I'd always been able to express myself to him. Frank sat in his chair with his hands interlocked, looking me dead in my eyes.

"Tell me, Lavelle, who was really the last to touch my money?" The distance in his voice let me know what he was thinking. This mothafucka was crazy. I knew he wasn't asking me that shit. I looked at him like he was outta his damn mind.

"First let me ask, are you accusing me of something?" I asked, wanting him to ask me straight out if I was stealing his money. "Don't dance around shit when you coming at me. Say what the fuck you mean and mean what the fuck you say. If you wanna ask something, ask me straight out. Don't beat around the fuckin' bush," I said, letting his ass know I wasn't for no games.

"There's no bitch in me nigga. I asked you a direct fucking question, and I want a straight answer. Who was really the last person to touch my money?" he asked with more bass in his voice than I cared for.

"I don't fuckin' know. Maurice offered to put the shit in the car. I gave the cases to him. I didn't touch any of the cases until he brought them in here to you." Frank sat back in his chair and began to nod. He looked like he was in deep thought.

"Well, I guess that's it, huh," he said with a flat voice. It was not really as a question, but more of a statement.

"That's it, that's why you called me here interrupting my family time?" I asked. For some reason, I felt like he was still accusing me of something.

"No! We need to discuss business. I think we need to change the set-up and the way things are run around here. First, we might be ending business with Rojas. I can't have my money coming short no more. We didn't have these types of problems until we started dealing with Rojas. I have a new connect that I am considering doing business with. He's offering his product at a better price. I need you to meet with him to see what he's talking about. I need someone I can really trust on this, and I want the deal pronto. You know how I hate for my time to be wasted." Frank was tense.

"I got you, Frank. I'll find out everything and let you know." I said. He nodded.

"I need to take a few days to let shit simmer for a bit before I decide on anything. I got to get some shit cleared up. I just need to figure out who on my team I can trust."

"Ok, be easy Frank, don't let this shit get to you. We will figure it out."

"Nigga, I'm cool as a muthafuckin' fan." he joked. "I'm not new to this. I have zero tolerance for disloyalty. None. So cleaning house is something that gotta be done, even if it hurts," he continued as he gave me a smirk. "Let yourself out and lock my shit behind you." he said, giving his usual handshake.

On the way to Mom's house, Adonis was rambling on about his situation. How in the fuck did he get that bitch Raquel and Venus pregnant at the same time? Then to find out on the same day? That shit was crazy. This nigga was sitting in the passenger seat looking like a lost puppy worried that Venus was gonna be done with his ass for real this time, and I wouldn't blame her. I didn't know what had been going on in this nigga's head lately, but he'd been doing some real fucked up shit when it came to her.

"Man, what the fuck am I gon' do?" he whined, rubbing his hands over his head.

"Nigga, I don't know what the fuck you gon' do." I replied. Honestly, I needed to sit this nigga down and tell him about himself, but right now I couldn't focus on him—not with this shit going on with Frank. I really thought the nigga was tryna low-key accuse me of stealing his shit.

Moms was too excited to see us. She jumped up and down, hugging us tightly and kissing all over our faces like she hadn't seen a nigga in a long ass time. The smell of the food was making my stomach growl; I was starving like shit. I didn't eat all day because I knew Moms was in the kitchen throwing down, and a nigga was making sure he could eat like muthafuckin' king. Mom prepared a Sunday dinner like the dinner they had on the movie Soul Food. Fried chicken, greens, baked macaroni and cheese, ham, and roast; shit, she cooked like it was Thanksgiving or something. That damn mac-n-cheese was on point like shit. We sat at the table, said grace, then started talking about what was going on in each other's life— the short version, of course. I tried to enjoy myself but something about my meeting with Frank didn't sit too well with me, and I couldn't get it off my mind.

After dinner, I sat down with Adonis in the family room and told him about the meeting with Frank. He felt the same way I was feeling. Frank was asking me if I was stealing. I couldn't believe that. I was the most loyal person that nigga ever had on his team. That was why he made me his right-hand. That was why we had the relationship that we had. Fuck I look like biting the hand that fed me?

"Man look, you need to look at Maurice. That nigga dirty, I'm telling you." Adonis spoke in a tone that let me know that he was dead ass.

"Maurice is Frank's son. He already got bread, why would he steal from Frank?" I asked, thinking that maybe Adonis was right. Maurice was the last that I knew to touch the money. I wasn't convinced and I didn't want to falsely accuse the nigga. Adonis' phone started ringing and he put his finger up telling me to wait a second. It was Venus telling him that Harmony wanted to talk to him. While waiting for her to give Harmony the phone, he put it on mute.

"All I'm saying is watch his bitch ass." He unmuted his phone, then gave Harmony his full attention. I sat there tryna put some pieces together in my own mind. I really thought all the hits that had been going on over the last few months and the money coming short was all done in-house, and I was gonna get to the bottom of it.

We left Mom's house and were headed to a bar so we could really talk this shit out. I needed for this shit to come to an end before I had to body the whole fuckin' crew—Frank included. Plus, I needed to get in Adonis' shit about his fucked up ass situation. Ain't no way in hell Venus was gonna fuck with his ass after this. He might as well take that fuckin' engagement ring back to Shad and get his fuckin' fifteen thousand dollars back, or get some shit for Harmony. The ringing phone got my attention. It was the call I had been waiting for.

"Yeah." I answered.

"Can we meet now?"

"Yeah, where at?"

"The usual."

"Aight, I'm not too far now. Be there in a few."

I hung up and told Adonis that I had to make a quick stop and I needed him to wait in the car for me. He nodded his head in agreement, but the distant look on his face let me know that he was in his head and wasn't paying attention to what I was saying. Fuck it, the nigga was in the passenger seat. He had no choice but the ride with me and wait in the car.

I pulled into the vacant lot behind an old, secluded condemned building that put me in the mind of a classic horror movie. I found the darkest spot that I could find and parked. I didn't want anyone to see my car or Adonis. I turned the car off and took the key out of the ignition. Adonis unbuckled his seat belt and reached for the door handle, but I stopped him.

"Stay in the car." I demanded.

"Nigga, it's dark as fuck out here, I can't see shit," he complained.

"Look, I need you to trust me and stay in the car." I gave him a look to let him know that my demand was non-negotiable.

"Aight nigga, damn; what the fuck we here for anyway?" he asked. I didn't respond.

I got my gun, put it in my waist, and headed to the front of the condemned building. I walked in and Anfernee, one of the workers, was tied to a chair blindfolded and gagged. I snatched the blindfold off and the nigga looked like his whole life had just passed before his eyes.

"You stealing money from us, nigga?" I asked as I towered over him, ready to do some more damage to his already busted up face. He didn't respond. I started raining blows on him. I had to take it a little easy. I knew his lil' bitch ass was working alone; he didn't have the heart to be the mastermind behind this shit. I hit him a few more times, then I needed him to talk.

"Anfernee, Anfernee, Anfernee, you really wanna give your life up for a nigga that wouldn't do the same for you? That nigga out here looking out for his fuckin' self. You were just a pawn in his game. You might as well make this easy on yourself; who the fuck are you working for?" I asked, elevating my voice to put fear in the nigga's heart. He jumped so quick that he almost fell out of the chair. He was breathing hard like he was about to cry, trembling and sweating and shit. I pulled out a knife and pressed under his eye. His breathing became labored as he let out a muffled yell. I removed the gag from his mouth.

"Scream all you want; no one can hear you in here. Now, this is the last time that I'm gonna ask you." I pressed the knife deeper into the skin under his eye. "Who the fuck is you working for?"

His wide eyes darted around the room as if he was begging for somebody to help him. I exhaled a frustrated breath. The look I was giving him must have alerted him to the fact that I was about to cut his eye out because he started to talk. His faint voice started cracking as he whispered the name. I didn't hear him, so I leaned closer and told him to repeat himself. His voice was slightly above a whisper as he called out.

POW! POW! POW!

To Be Continued.

Interested in becoming a part of the Treasured Publications family?

Submit manuscripts to

Info@Treasuredpub.com

Like us on Facebook:

Treasured Publications

Be sure to text **Treasured** to **22828**

To subscribe to our Mailing List.

Never miss a release or contest

again!

CPSIA information can be obtained at www.ICGtesting.com
Printed in the USA
LVOW10s2123080916

503790LV00030B/659/P